TARJEN

Star-Crossed Alien Mail Order Brides

SUSAN HAYES

ABOUT THE BOOK

What do you do when your planet runs out of women? Send for takeout, of course.

Tarjen never expected to go to Earth again. The first time, he was there to protect Crown Prince Joran as he claimed his mate and returned her to Pyros. This time, Tarjen is on his way to claim a mate of his own.

He's studied human courtship behaviour, memorized his match's file from the Star-Crossed Dating database, and prepared himself for the moment he'll meet his mate. He's planned everything perfectly so that nothing can go wrong. Not like the last time they were here...

This book contains a single mother who doesn't believe in happy endings, and a royal bodyguard who does everything by the book – until the universe blows up the book, his plans, and part of a city block.

SUSAN HAYES

Tarjen (Book #4 of the Star-crossed Alien Mail Order Brides Series)

First E-book Publication: September 2018

Cover Design: crocodesigns.com

Editor: Dayna Hart

Published by: Black Scroll Publications

ISBN: 978-1-988446-32-5

As always, this story is dedicated to my Mum and Dad, for their love and support of their sometimes-crazy daughter, and to Karen, the "sister of my heart."

This one also goes out to my readers. When I started this series, I had no idea how it would be received. Thank you for loving these stories so that I can continue to write them!

CHAPTER ONE

ARIA NEVER STOOD A CHANCE. Hell, she didn't even see it coming. The first she knew of the attack was when the gooey gob of applesauce landed on her cheek. "Melody, no! We don't throw food at mommy."

Her baby responded with giggles and a sticky-faced smile.

"It's amazing. She can't navigate the distance from the bowl to her mouth without dropping half her meal, but she somehow managed to hit you square in the face from halfway across the room." Haley's expression was a mix of amusement and horror. It was a common expression for the always-polished journalist when she was around Melody. Haley adored the little girl, but nothing in her world had prepared her for the chaos and mess that came with having a baby around.

"She's very talented." Aria Frasier managed to wipe off most of the applesauce from her cheek with a few swipes of the cloth she'd planned to use to clean

Melody with once she was finished her meal. She tossed it across the room, banking it off a cabinet door and into a basket she kept in a relatively uncluttered corner, where it joined the rest of her ever-growing stack of baby-related laundry.

"More proof that she takes after her mommy and not her jackass of a father." Haley filled both their wine glasses before adding, "And I know I'm not supposed to badmouth Danny in front of the sprout. I had a spectacularly bad week and my filters are all broken. Sorry."

"You're forgiven. I know it's been a bad week if you come straight here instead of heading home to change first."

"On a scale of one-to-ten, this week was a negative forty."

"Do you want to talk about what happened?" Aria asked.

Haley shook her head hard enough her perfect auburn curls bounced. "It's nothing new. Dad is still pushing me to prove myself, whatever the hell that means, and Mom is determined to find me a new husband. When I try and tell her I'm not ready, she gives me this confused look, like I'm not speaking English, and goes right back to reciting the income and suitability of the men she's found for me."

"I'm sorry. Some people refuse to accept that grief doesn't have a timetable. And your father..." she sighed. "I've got a degree in psychology and I still can't figure out what he wants from you."

Haley laughed. "It's nice to know I'm not the only one. Honestly, I don't think Dad knows what he wants from me, either. He's still angry I married Jeff, but now I'm a widow and he doesn't know how to punish me for my choice without being a monster."

"He's still being a jerk," Aria muttered as she cleared away the remains of Melody's meal and set some of her toys on the tray to keep her busy.

"Is that your professional opinion?" Haley teased.

"Nope. My professional opinion would use multisyllabic words and come with a bill. This is just me, talking as your friend. And your friend thinks he's being an A-S-S-H-O-L-E."

Haley snorted. "How long before your sprout learns to spell and that tactic doesn't work anymore?"

"Not long enough. She's starting to mimic what she hears, too, and Piper has even fewer filters than you do. With my luck, my little girl will be swearing like a trucker by the time she gets to pre-school." The mere thought of Melody heading to pre-school was enough to have Aria taking several drinks from her glass.

"You okay?" Haley asked.

"Yeah. I'm just not ready to think about Melody in school. I still feel like I only brought her home from the hospital yesterday."

"Time passes, whether we want it to or not." There was a rare note of sadness in Haley's voice. She had built up thick emotional walls since losing her husband, and it wasn't often she let anyone see past the carefully crafted veneer of a polished and professional career woman.

"Yes, it does." Aria leaned down to press a kiss to Melody's forehead. "I just wish I could capture these moments somehow, so I could visit them later, you know?"

Haley set her elbows on the battered kitchen table and nodded. "But as my wise and all- knowing therapist would say, the past is a tempting trap. The longer you linger in memories, the harder it is to come back."

Aria wrinkled her nose and recklessly drained her glass. "Please tell me I didn't actually say that."

"I might have adlibbed a little."

Aria reached for the wine bottle. "Thank god. That sounded like it came out of a fortune cookie."

She barely got a splash of wine into the bottom of her glass before the kitchen door was flung open and Piper exploded into the room. "Email!"

"Manners!" Aria shot back.

Piper rolled her eyes and stuck her tongue out, revealing the piercing Aria had forbidden her to get back when she was a teenager. She came to a skidding halt by Melody, gave the baby a loud kiss on the cheek, and dropped into the nearest chair.

"This is important. Did you read your email lately, or have you been too busy drinking all the wine before I got here?"

"I haven't checked it lately. Unlike you, I'm capable of putting my phone down for—"

"Yeah, yeah. I'm an addict. I need to look up and see the world sometimes. I know the speech by heart. This is important, though! Check it out, I got an invite to the Star-Crossed Dating Agency gathering at the end of next month." She tucked a lock of blue hair behind her ear, unlocked her phone, and then waved it around too fast for anyone to be able to read what was on the screen.

"The alien dating agency? You signed up for that?" Haley gawked at Piper.

"Well, at the time it was just another online dating site. Remember, sis? We signed up together."

Aria remembered. It was only a week after she had discovered Danny was cheating on her. Piper had suggested they both sign up for the new online dating site, and Aria had consumed just enough wine and ice cream to think it was a good idea. "Wait a second. They sent me a refund and told me there was no match for me in their database. You got one, too. So how come you're getting an invite?"

"Who cares? I get to go see the alien hotties, and I bet you've got an invite, too." Piper bounded out of her chair again, snagged the wine bottle in one hand and went in search of a clean glass. "You look, while I pour."

It took a few minutes to track down her phone, and another minute or so to skim through her emails, looking for something from Star-Crossed. "I don't have an email from them."

"You sure?" Piper leaned over her shoulder and

peered at her phone. "That's your work email, goofball. Where's the personal account I set up for you just for online dating and stuff?"

"I forgot it existed." She handed the phone to Piper. "How do I access that other account?"

Piper tapped the screen a few times. "You managed to unlink your accounts. Here, I …holy shit!"

"Bit!" Melody repeated with a happy chortle.

Haley burst out laughing. "You're screwed, Ri."

"More than she knows." Piper handed over her phone.

"If this is bad news, I don't want to know."

"It's not bad. I think it's amazing. You…may not feel the same way."

Aria started reading. It wasn't an invitation to the gathering being held in Vancouver. It was… "Oh my god."

"What?!" Haley demanded.

"I have a match. A potential dating match. With one of them. The aliens." She was still reading and re-reading the opening lines of the email in disbelief.

"No way!" Haley got to her feet and hurried over to read over her shoulder. "Welcome to the most stellar dating experience of your life. Really? That's their sales pitch?"

"They don't need a sales pitch. These guys are all gorgeous. And they mate for life! No cheating." Piper picked Melody up out of the highchair and danced around the room with her. "You're going to have a daddy from outer space, baby girl!"

"Not likely. I signed up for this before I knew I was pregnant. No man wants to be stuck raising another man's baby." Aria pointed to the phone. "Besides, this email was sent a month ago. He'll have moved on by now."

"Don't you dare talk yourself out of this," Haley said.

"But he's an alien! What kind of father could he be?"

"You should at least look before you reject him. You have to be open to change, remember, oh wise one?"

Aria groaned. "You're using my own advice against me?"

"Damn right. Now click the link."

Piper started chanting. "Click the link. Click the link!"

"I haven't even read the whole email, yet." Flustered, she tried to scroll down to keep reading, but her fingers, still sticky with applesauce residue, stuck to the screen and left a smear across the glass. "Dammit." She tried again, but instead of scrolling down, a new screen opened, displaying a photo of a man too hot to be real. He had to be photoshopped.

He looked like he was wearing a uniform of some kind, the black fabric cut in crisp, sharp lines that only enhanced his hard, lean body. He had short brown hair and dark, serious eyes, but his smile was earnest, almost boyish.

"Oh, wow," Haley murmured. "Is that your match?"

"Uh. I think so."

She tried to scroll down to his details, but her finger

got stuck again. Right over the button that read "Accept Match."

A digitized burst of fireworks exploded across her screen, and the word "Congratulations" flashed several times. It was replaced by a scrolling bit of text in bright red. "Welcome to Star-Crossed dating service. Your mating adventure starts today!"

"Shit! No, no, no. Where's the undo button?"

'What did you do?" Piper asked.

"Shbit!" Melody babbled, caught up in everyone's excitement.

"My fat finger hit the accept button! Dammit, how do I take it back?"

"Let me see." Piper handed Aria her daughter and then took the phone from her.

"First of all, let me say that as accidental mates go, you won the lottery. He's gorgeous!"

"Not helping, Pi. Just fix it. Please." She hugged Melody tight.

"I don't think I can. There's no undo option."

Haley straightened. "That can't be right. They can't make Aria marry some random alien just because she clicked a link. That's entrapment."

Aria recognized the shift in her friend's tone. Haley smelled a story. "No one is going to *make* me marry anyone. From what I've read, these aliens—"

"Pyrosians," Piper corrected, looking up from the screen for a moment.

"These Pyrosians are decent enough. They'll understand there's been a mistake."

"I'm not sure it's going to be that simple. I read the information, and there's no way to contact your match until he arrives here on Earth. Something about Earth lacking the technology to communicate over the distance required." Piper handed the phone back to Aria. "On the plus side, this means you'll be coming to the Gathering with me. You can explain it to them, or to him. His name is Tarjen, by the way. Maybe if you meet him…"

Aria scoffed and poked at her squishy stomach. "What? That handsome hunk of alien male is going to take one look at me in all my pudgy splendor and decide he can't live without me?"

"If he's got eyes in his head, then yes, he will. You're beautiful, inside and out. I wish you could see that." Piper poured them all more wine.

"I'm just being realistic. There's no point in getting myself worked up over something that is never going to happen. We'll go to this Gathering, I'll explain, and then we'll come home."

Haley cleared her throat. "Does that invitation say anything about bringing a guest?"

"Looking to score a husband that would send your parents into orbit?" Piper asked. "I think I can bring a guest, yeah."

"I'm looking for a story that will finally impress my father, and I think I've found it," Haley declared.

Aria sighed and kissed Melody's forehead. "Want to go meet some aliens, baby girl?"

Melody cooed and bopped the phone with one pudgy fist.

"Don't you start. You're too young to date."

THE DOOR to the crown prince's office slid open and Tarjen snapped to attention, assuming that Crown Prince Joran and his princess were on their way to their next engagement. Instead, he was summoned inside.

"Senior Guardsman Tarjen Rix, I need a word with you. Now," The prince's normally mellow voice was unusually sharp.

He nodded to the guard standing next to him, pivoted sharply on one heel, and entered the office. He had no idea what Joran wanted of him, but judging by his tone, it was important. He saluted the prince and princess, right arm across his chest, palm over his heart, then came to attention. "Yes, Highness?"

The door closed, and the moment they were alone, the atmosphere changed. Joran rose from behind his desk of smoked glass and polished metal, his serious expression morphing into a broad grin.

Maggie uttered a joyful laugh. She was already standing, one hand resting on the curve of her pregnant stomach. "Breathe, Tarjen. It's good news!"

"I don't understand. I'm not expecting any news." He looked at the two of them in confusion. Beyond them, the window displayed a breathtaking view of the palace grounds and city that lay beyond it.

"Can I tell him?" Maggie asked.

"Of course, *seska*." The prince smiled and nodded to his human mate. Tarjen envied them their closeness but having been there at the beginning of their relationship, he knew it had taken work to get to here.

"Star-Crossed has located a match for you on Earth!" Maggie was almost vibrating with excitement as she shared the news.

Tarjen's heart skipped a beat. "What?" He couldn't speak more than a single syllable, but inside his head, his thoughts were whizzing around like a meteor swarm. The Gods had granted him a mate! Flames and fury, it didn't seem possible.

"You have a potential mate waiting for you on Earth. Her acceptance of the match only came through this morning. Her name is Aria. She's even from Vancouver, the same city where Joran found me. I'll send you her file as soon as you're off duty."

He blew out a breath and looked from Maggie to Joran. "A human female? For me?" He was still struggling to believe it. He had come to accept that he would never experience the joy of the mating bond. Female births had diminished to the point that the Pyrosian species was at risk of extinction. Even after the discovery of potential mates on the distant planet Earth, he hadn't expected to claim a mate. Only the prince and a handful of young males from rich, powerful families had been permitted on that first desperate journey.

Joran came over to stand in front of him, all decorum forgotten as he slapped Tarjen on the shoulder as if they were both fellow soldiers again. "Congratulations, my friend. I hope you are as happy as I am with my Earth-born mate."

Maggie laughed. "And I hope you have a better first meeting than when Joran met me."

"I'm not likely to ditch my guards and run off to meet my match before I was supposed to. When I make a plan, I do not deviate from it." He gave his friend a playful smile. "Unlike a certain prince we both know."

"It worked out in the end," Joran protested.

"Only because I am a patient, forgiving woman." Maggie joined them, slipping her arm around her mate and leaning into his side.

"I would ask a favour of you, if I might, Princess?" Tarjen asked.

"Please tell me you're going to ask me for dating advice. I would love to help you woo your match!"

Her response didn't surprise Tarjen. Maggie had a kind and generous spirit that had won over even the most doubting minds among his race. "I would appreciate any help you could give me. I intend to broom this female off her feet and give her every reason to accept our bonding."

"You mean you're going to *sweep* her off her feet," Maggie corrected. "My first bit of advice is to refresh your English language skills with more cognitive augmentation, especially the idioms and slang terms. We've prepared new programs for all the males heading to Earth to meet their matches. This time, everyone will be better prepared, and the females will know better what they've signed up for." She frowned slightly. "But they won't know everything."

Joran hugged his mate. "You know why it has to be this way."

"I do. That doesn't mean I agree with it. You'll still have some explaining to do, Tarjen. Be gentle with her."

He nodded, already starting to make plans. There was so much to prepare for, and not much time to get it all done. "I'll do that tonight, once I am off-duty. In fact, I will make a list of everything that I need to do before we depart."

"I'll have someone over at Star-Crossed send you an information package. It should help," Maggie offered.

Tarjen saluted again, his chest swelling with unexpected emotions. He was going to be a mated male! "Thank you, highnesses. You have no idea what this means to me."

"I think I do, my friend." Joran squeezed his shoulder again before stepping away.

Tarjen glanced at Maggie, who was smiling at Joran like he was the center of the galaxy. One day soon, he would have a female who looked at him that way. "Thank you. It's thanks to you and your friends that males like me are now permitted to seek matches with the females of your planet. To be one of the males matched…It is an honour and a gift without price." He bowed his head. "I will be forever in your debt, Your Highness."

Maggie's expression softened. "If you want to impress Aria, all you have to do is say things like that."

"I can do that." He'd do whatever it took. Tonight, he would memorize her file to learn everything he could about her. Her likes and dislikes, her favourite foods, her hobbies. Then, he'd formulate a plan. She may be his destined mate, but Tarjen intended to give Aria every reason to choose him willingly. He'd seen firsthand what happened when human females were denied a choice, and he had no intention of repeating the mistakes of the last mission. This time would be different.

CHAPTER TWO

Aria was surrounded by women. Some of them were eagerly bouncing in place, peering about, trying to catch a glimpse of the aliens they had come to see. Others looked uneasy, tugging at their clothes and toying with their hair or their jewellery. There were very few men around, and most of them were wearing security badges and uniforms. It didn't make her feel any safer.

"There's an awful lot of security here." Haley was surreptitiously snapping pictures with her phone as they stood in line, waiting for their turn to show their identification and invitations.

The invites had arrived in the mail two weeks ago, a simple but elegantly embossed white invitation for Piper, and a more ornate, crimson and gold one for Aria. They were both marked with a barcode, and from what Aria could see, the guards were scanning each one and comparing names to a list before allowing each guest to pass. Aria gripped her invitation tight and asked herself the same question she'd been asking since they had arrived. *What the hell am I doing here?*

"Yeah, it's probably because of the anti-alien sentiment," Piper said. She had Melody in a baby sling and was distracting her with funny faces as they waited in the summer sunshine.

"What anti-alien sentiment?" Aria demanded. "The news hasn't mentioned anything about that."

Piper rolled her eyes. "You really need to spend more time online and less time reading the dead-tree scrolls delivered to our door every morning. It's all over Twitter. There are groups that are totally against human women hooking up with aliens and leaving the planet. Unsurprisingly, they're mostly made up of men who couldn't get a date to save their lives but have somehow convinced themselves it's because aliens are stealing all the women."

"Hey, I work for one of those *dead-tree scrolls*, you whippersnapper. Show some respect for the newspaper industry, will you?" Haley retorted.

"You only work for your dad's company because you haven't decided what you want to be when you grow up." Piper said, then turned her attention to Melody. "You're not going to have that problem, are you? You're going to be a chef when you grow up, right, sprout? You're going to be just like your Aunt Piper, only with better luck picking places to work."

Sensing a much-needed distraction, Aria turned to

look at her sister. "What's wrong with your new job? I thought you didn't even start until next week."

"Not anymore." Piper managed a lopsided smile that didn't reach her eyes. "I got a call while you were getting ready. There was an issue with the new wiring they installed. It caused a fire. A *big* fire. There's nothing left of the Root and Vine but rubble and ash."

"Oh no! Will they rebuild? Do you still have a job? Why didn't you say anything sooner?" Aria wrapped her sister in a hug, being careful not to squish Melody in the process.

"I didn't say anything because I knew you'd do this."

"Do what?" Aria asked.

"Overreact," Piper hissed the word as she pulled away.

"I'm not overreacting. This is terrible news. Do you need to talk about it?"

Piper held up a hand. "Ri, stop it. I'm fine. Well, no, I'm not fine, but I will be eventually."

Aria ached for her sister. Piper had worked hard to get to this point in her career, and to have it literally burn down around her was so unfair. Aria wanted to be there for her, but Piper was already pushing her away. It was a dynamic they couldn't seem to shake, no matter how hard Aria tried. This wasn't the time to talk about it, though. She redirected the conversation instead. "What happens now?"

Piper shrugged. "The owners are still trying to figure things out. They sunk everything they had into this renovation. I guess it all depends on their insurance. And yeah, they said I've still got the job as head chef if I want it, but they don't know when, or if, they'll be reopening."

"Do you want me to ask around and see if anyone knows of an opening for a chef?" Haley asked.

"That would be great, thanks. It's too early to know what's going to happen, but it can't hurt to start putting out feelers in case it's a worst-case scenario." Piper smiled at Haley before looking straight at Aria and raising a finger in warning. "And that's the last I want to hear about me. This is *your* day, not mine."

"You mean it's my day to tell an alien who travelled light-years to meet me that it's all a mistake because I hit a button I shouldn't have?"

Piper's eyes narrowed. "You're still determined to say no? What if you two have that spark thing they mentioned?"

"There has to be contact to initiate the Spark. Once we meet face to face I don't think that's going to happen. You've seen Tarjen's picture. He can do so much better."

Haley grumbled under her breath, then reached out to flick the sleeve of the cranberry red sundress Aria wore. "If that's how you see this going, then why did you go all out? Hair, make-up--you're even wearing your only pair of non-sensible shoes."

"It was an excuse to dress up. I don't get many of those anymore."

Haley arched a brow. "Uh huh. I don't believe that's

the only reason. Your sister's right. Don't be too quick to say no. You deserve good things, Aria. Believe that."

"I have Melody. That's enough."

"You deserve someone who will make you and Melody the center of his world. Good. Kind. Caring. All the things that Danny pretended to be but wasn't." Haley said.

"You're always taking care of other people. Me, your patients, your daughter. You should have someone in your life who wants to take care of you." Piper grinned and tossed her hair, making it shimmer blue-green in the sunlight. "And no, I don't count. Though I *am* the world's most amazing sister."

They kept to lighter topics after that, and before long they were just a few feet from the security checkpoint. Once they passed through, Piper and Haley would be directed toward the seating area, while Aria would be sent to join the other matches. "We're nearly there. I should take Melody."

Piper sighed. "Are you sure you don't want me to keep her? It would make your meeting less awkward."

"I'm sure." Aria held out her hands and Piper expertly transferred both baby and sling over to Aria. It took a few minutes to get everything in place, and by then, they were in front of the guards. She and Piper offered their invitations, which were scanned and cross-checked. Haley produced her driver's license, verifying she was the person named as Piper's plus one. No one said anything about Melody.

She'd half-expected them to turn her away right

there and then, but instead they waved her through and directed her toward a group of women, all wearing some sort of official badge. "One of the guides will escort you, ma'am. Good luck today."

Haley stopped to hug her. "Keep your heart open," was all she said.

"I love you. Be fierce. Trust your instincts." Piper gave her a one-armed hug and then grinned at her. "Go get yourself an alien hottie."

A moment later they were gone and she was standing in the entryway to B.C. Place Stadium with her daughter, a diaper bag, and a strong urge to bolt back out onto the street.

A bright-eyed blonde wearing one of the badges appeared at her elbow and smiled in welcome. "Hi. You're one of the lucky matches, aren't you? Why don't you follow me and I'll take you to your seat?"

"I uh, yes please." She snuck a peek at the woman's badge. "Thank you, Eva. I'm feeling a bit lost."

"You're not alone. I've seen the same expression on a lot of faces today." She glanced down at Melody. "You just hang onto your little girl and remember to breathe."

"I'll try." Aria followed the pert volunteer along a series of hallways. The bustle and hum of the crowd outside fell away, but soon she could hear a different noise coming from up ahead. They went through a wide tunnel and stepped out onto the floor of the stadium.

"Wow," she muttered as they stepped into the huge, sunlit space.

"You think this is wow, wait until you meet the Pyrosians. They're gorgeous. Every single one of them." Eva gave a wistful sigh and touched a spot over her heart. "And they're so eager to meet their matches, it's enough to make your heart melt. I know you're nervous, but from what I've seen, these guys are worth the risk. I'd give almost anything to be able to try for one of them."

"Why can't you?" Aria asked.

"They need to rebuild their population, and I can't have kids." Eva reached over to stroke Melody's cheek. "I'm not what they're looking for, but you are. Whoever your match is, I bet he can't wait to meet you and this little sweetheart."

The truth tumbled out of her mouth before she knew she was going to speak at all. "He doesn't know. About Melody, I mean. I signed up before I knew I was pregnant. There's no way…"

"You think this is going to make one of them change their minds? Oh honey, no. I've been working with these guys for days setting everything up. Trust me, your match is going to be thrilled."

Eva checked her tablet as Aria looked around. She'd been in B.C. Place Stadium before, but only for concerts. Standing in the middle of everything, with the roof open overhead and the sunlight streaming into the vast space was a very different experience. Broad awnings shaded the tiers of seats that ringed the stadium, keeping the sun off the spectators. Large white, open-walled tents had been set up over the seating for the women, and there were enough floral arrangements around the tents and the dais to evoke the image of an outdoor wedding.

"Got it. You're in the front row, just over here." Eva was almost bouncing as she led Aria to her seat. "You'll have a perfect view of all the proceedings from here."

There were only a few spaces left in her section, and all the women already seated were giving her nervous smiles of welcome. "Thank you."

Eva patted her arm. "Good luck today. I think your match is a lucky man -- er, alien."

Aria took her seat and settled her daughter on her lap. A quick check of her phone told her there were still about thirty minutes before the event was scheduled to begin. More and more of the stadium seats were filling up as she watched. After a few minutes, men in black uniforms started moving around the stage, checking equipment and talking to each other in a language she didn't recognize. Were they Pyrosians? They looked human enough, but then again, so did Tarjen, at least in his picture.

Was he here already? He must be, but so far, she hadn't seen more than a few of his people around. She felt a pang of guilt. Eva said the men were all eager to meet their matches. Until now, she'd managed to convince herself that Tarjen wouldn't want this any more than she did. What if she was wrong?

She bowed her head over Melody's. "I have to do what's best for you, sweetheart, but right now, I'm not sure what that is."

Melody tugged on a lock of Aria's hair. "Bit!" she announced.

Aria couldn't help but laugh. "You got that right."

TARJEN WASN'T USED to being away from his prince at events like this. He was part of Joran's honour guard, sworn to protect and defend the future ruler of his planet. He should be at Joran's side, ensuring that both the crown prince and his princess were safe. Instead, he was with the other matched males waiting impatiently for their cue to enter the stadium and begin the Gathering.

This wasn't a Gathering in the traditional sense. The days of bringing together hundreds of young Pyrosians to meet in hopes of initiating a Spark and finding their true mate had ended generations ago. As science advanced, the matching process had become a matter of comparing information in a database and sending the results to the pair destined to be mates.

Maggie and the other human females wanted to bring back some of the pageantry of those long-ago days. When he'd asked Joran why, he had learned it was less about nostalgia and more about appearances. The governments might have agreed to exchange Pyrosian technology and information for human females, but not everyone on Earth agreed with the decision. This entire event was designed to foster goodwill and acceptance.

It was also the moment that his entire life would change.

"How much longer?" someone muttered from behind him.

"Too damned long," someone else responded.

He agreed with the sentiment, even though he understood the need to wait. They wouldn't start the procession until the shuttle holding Joran, Maggie and the rest of the high-ranking guests were in position and had final clearance to land. Until then, the matched males were waiting in several rooms and staging areas around the arena. When they got the signal, they would march to their seats in formation as the shuttle descended into the arena via the open roof.

It had been Maggie and Gwen's idea for all of them to be wearing matching garments made for this occasion. It was similar enough to his usual uniform to feel familiar, but it lacked something important. He was unarmed, and the lack of a weapon made him uneasy. He'd included almost every other item in his usual kit, but he'd been ordered not to bring his sidearm. Not that he expected to need it, but what if something went wrong? He'd been to Earth before. The inhabitants were volatile and occasionally violent. Many humans were still ruled by their fears.

He couldn't wait to get Aria on board the *Firebrand*. She'd be safe there, and safer still once they returned to Pyros. He wouldn't be able to offer her riches or power, but he would ensure that she was cherished and protected every day for the rest of her life.

The door to their area opened and an upbeat blonde woman appeared and spoke to them in English. "It's almost time. Your matches are all out there, waiting for you. Every single one of them."

There was a collective sigh of relief from around the room.

"I'll be giving you the signal to start in less than a minute. Good luck." She smiled at them and then switched to Pyrosian. "May the gods bless you all on this day."

Around him, everyone checked their clothes and hair one last time. Tarjen focused on another set of details. He had his welcoming words to Aria memorized. His room back on the *Firebrand* was stocked with a wide variety of human delicacies that he'd arranged to be transported to the ship already. He had researched courting rituals for her species and tried to follow as many of them as he could. There were chocolates and several dozen roses, and in his pocket was a ring set with a golden gem from the mountains of Pyros.

He went over his mental checklist one more time and smiled to himself. He was as prepared as he could possibly be.

"It's go time. File out in order, find your seat, and remember to smile!" The blonde opened the double doors and stepped out of the way.

It was a short walk to the open air of the stadium, but it felt like they were marching forever by the time they reached the end of the tunnel and he stepped out into the dazzling sunlight.

Applause and cheers erupted as they emerged, the noise so deafening Tarjen felt the ground beneath him vibrating. The royal shuttle was already descending, and he had a stab of guilt that he wasn't onboard with the rest of Joran's guards. Today, that wasn't his mission, he reminded himself. Today, his mission was Aria.

He scanned the area where the human females were already seated, and his heart leaped as he spotted Aria seated right up front. He knew it was her. He had memorized her face from the pictures in her file. What none of those pictures had shown was the child she was holding. Was it hers? Was his mate already claimed by another? What little social media presence his mate had was focused on her work as a counsellor. There had been almost no mention of her personal life, and the governments of Earth had forbidden the Pyrosians from prying too much into the female's private lives.

The roar of the crowd grew exponentially louder, and the ground shifted again. A shockwave slammed into him, pushing him forward as the cheers of welcome turned to terrified screams, and the stadium erupted into chaos.

He took off at a run for the last place he'd seen Aria. He had to get to her. Had to protect her.

As he ran, he caught sight of the shuttle hurtling up and away from whatever insanity was unfolding around him. Another explosion nearly knocked him off his feet, and the ringing in his ears blocked out the screams of fear and pain. He pushed through the panicked crowd, looking for Aria. Other males were doing the same thing, but there were fewer of them than there should have been. He'd been in battle before. He knew what lay behind him: carnage and destruction. He didn't look back. He couldn't. He had to find her.

There! He caught sight of her red dress and veered toward it. She was caught up in a crowd of human females darting around like a flock of frightened birds. He lost her again and ran blindly through the crowd, hoping to find her before anything else happened.

An ear-shattering roar tore through the stadium, and a massive winged shape took to the air. Vadir's Romaki guest, Prince Radek, must have shifted forms, despite his vow not to.

He caught another flash of red and forgot about Radek and his broken promises. She'd managed to break free of the crowd and was ducking into a tunnel much like the one he'd walked through a few minutes ago. He sprinted after her, calling her name.

She disappeared into the tunnel, and then there was a brilliant flash of light and another explosion, this one close enough the force sent him flying backward. He hit the ground hard but was on his feet in seconds. He couldn't hear anything, and his vision was marred by the afterimages of the explosion, but he staggered toward the tunnel entrance. Only the entrance wasn't there anymore. Huge chunks of concrete tumbled into the space, forming a barricade.

"Flames and fury!" he cursed. There was only one way to reach Aria now. He shoved up the sleeve of his shirt, uncovering the teleportation device he'd strapped to his wrist before leaving his quarters. It was programmed to take him back to the safety of a nearby shuttle in case of emergency. This was definitely an emergency, but he had no intention of returning to the ship without Aria. He'd made a plan, and by the Gods, he wasn't going to let anything stop him from completing it.

He adjusted the coordinates, doublechecked them, and squared his shoulders. He had to find his mate. Once he did that, he'd be able to introduce himself.

That was the next step in his plan, and it would take more than a few explosions to stop that from happening. He hit the final key and braced himself for the unpleasant sensations that always accompanied teleportation. It would be worth it though, once he found Aria and made sure she was safe.

CHAPTER THREE

"This is the last time we listen to your Aunt Piper," Aria crooned to her baby, trying to keep her tone light, despite the insanity surrounding them. There was no pattern to the explosions, no way to know which direction led to safety, so she'd chosen at random. When the crowd engulfed her, she had pushed through them. There was no safety to be found in numbers.

Melody was wailing in fear, and Aria was tempted to wail along with her. Instead, she held tight to her little girl and hurried across the stadium floor toward an entrance identical to the one Eva had taken her through. It had to be a way out. Chunks of concrete and debris were strewn across the ground, forcing her to move slower than she would have liked. If only she'd been smart and worn her sensible shoes, she'd be outside by now.

A terrible noise tore through the air behind her, and she bolted the last few feet into the tunnel. Once she made it inside there was no more debris, so she kept running, desperate to get clear of the destruction. Once she was outside, she could start looking for Piper and Haley.

She only got a few meters before there was another explosion. This one was close enough it shook the ground and sent her tumbling forward, the shockwave almost lifting her off her feet. She hit the ground on her side, both arms wrapped around Melody.

There was a thunderous boom somewhere in the distance. All the lights flickered and then went out. She was alone in the dark.

Still winded by her fall, her senses scrambled, Aria forced herself back to her feet. Fear tried to take hold, but she pushed it back and made herself focus on the only thing that mattered. Melody. Her baby was a warm, comforting weight against her chest.

"You okay, little one?" She ran her hands over every inch of her child, soothing her as she checked for injuries. By the time she was done, Melody was quieter, and Aria breathed a sigh of relief. "No owies or booboos. Thank heavens."

She reached out one hand and started shuffling in a cautious circle, searching for a wall to use as a guide. She wandered for what felt like an eternity in the darkness, her nerves screaming, but finally her hand brushed against something solid.

"Thank god." She leaned her back against the wall and gave herself a moment. She was running on instinct and adrenaline. She needed to calm down and start thinking clearly. She took a few cleansing breaths, counting out the seconds of each exhalation. Just as she started feeling more centered, she heard something in the darkness, and fear turned her blood to ice water in a heartbeat. Who was out there? What was out there in the dark?

"Hello?"

"Aria? Are you unhurt?" A stranger's voice called out.

"Who are you? Where are you? I can't see anything."

A hand touched her shoulder and a brilliant blue spark arced through the air, chasing away the dark for a moment. Once she saw the spark, she knew exactly who was with her. Her Pyrosian match had tracked her down somehow, and now both of them would have to face the consequences. *I shouldn't have come today. He's going to be so disappointed.*

"Tarjen?"

A pale golden light filled the air, and she found herself staring into the face of her match. "Greetings, Aria of Earth. Thank the gods you are unhurt." He raised the hand holding the light source so he could see her better. "You are unhurt, yes? You and the child?"

"We're okay. This is Melody." She paused before adding. "My daughter." She expected Tarjen to pull away or say something dismissive. The last thing in the world she expected the tall, broad-shouldered male to do was to reach out and stroke a calloused finger over Melody's tiny hand.

"Greetings, Melody of Earth."

Melody grabbed his finger. "Bee-bee."

He frowned in confusion. "I do not know that expression."

"That's because the only one who knows what it means is Melody. She can't really talk yet, she's too young. I guess you don't have many children on your world, do you? I mean, with the lack of females and all…" She was babbling, but it was hard not to given the circumstances.

"Your daughter is beautiful, as are you." He gently removed his finger from Melody's grasp and pointed into the looming darkness. "I wish to talk with you, but first, we should get you and the little one to safety."

"I want to get out of here. I need to make sure my sister and my friend are safe, too. They were in the stands, watching. Do you think they're okay?"

Tarjen couldn't know any more than she did, but he placed a comforting hand on her shoulder and nodded. "We'll find them, *seska*."

She took a good look at the man who believed they were destined to be together forever. He looked much like his picture, though he was much bigger in person than she had expected. Seeing someone's height listed was one thing, but actually looking up at someone over six feet tall with shoulders as wide as his…that was another matter. It was crazy, but she caught herself wondering what he'd look like without his shirt. Was he as muscular and hard as he appeared? *What would he taste like when he kissed me?*

She slammed the brakes on that line of thinking. They needed to get out of here, and then she needed to tell him that it wasn't going to work. That she hadn't meant to accept the match. Of course, she had planned on telling him all of this before he touched her. *Before* the Spark had blazed between them, confirming their compatibility.

He led them down the tunnel, but it wasn't long before they could see that it was blocked by a pile of rubble.

"Is that the way you came in?" she asked.

He cocked his arm toward her, indicating a strange device strapped to his wrist. "I used a teleporter. It was the only way I could reach you."

"You have a teleporter? That's a thing?" She stared at the device in amazement. "So, you can just teleport us all out of here, right?"

He sighed and shook his head. "It's too dangerous to use it unless I know the exact coordinates and can confirm the location is clear. Plus, I'm not sure what it might do to Melody. The process is…unpleasant."

"Then we won't do it." She wouldn't risk hurting Melody. "Wait. If it's dangerous to teleport without knowing where you are going, how'd you get to us?"

Tarjen turned, his solemn gaze meeting hers. He reached up to cup her cheek, his thumb caressing her. "You are mine to protect, and I couldn't do that if I wasn't with you."

She stared up at him, shocked. "You risked being hurt to get to me? Why?"

He shrugged and leaned in closer. "You are my true mate, Aria. The one the Gods created to walk at my side. There is nothing I wouldn't do to ensure your safety, and your happiness."

"Tarjen—" Her words were cut off by a kiss so hot it turned all her arguments to ash in an instant. His mouth slanted over hers in an act of primal possession. His hand moved from her cheek to spear into her hair, sending the carefully placed bobby pins flying. He drew her in close, near enough she could feel the heat radiating off his body. He curved his big body around Melody, being careful not to crush her between them.

Aria gave in to desire and kissed him back. The instant she parted her lips, he growled low in his throat and took the kiss deeper. Need tore through her like wildfire and she rose on her toes to meet him, her hand gripping the fabric of his shirt. If another explosion had gone off at that moment, she wouldn't have noticed. His kiss was all-consuming, and his touch brought feeling back to parts of her body she had forgotten existed.

She was supposed to be telling him this was a mistake. That she wasn't the woman he was waiting for. But how the hell was she going to do that when she wasn't sure she believed it anymore?

Two thoughts crashed through Tarjen's mind as he kissed Aria for the first time. She was utterly perfect, and he didn't deserve her. Not that he'd let that fact stop him from claiming her. He'd seen the blue light of the Spark as it had arced between them. They were true mates. Soon, the Scorching would take hold of them, driving them into a mating fever that would last for at least two of Earth's solar cycles.

The fever was already affecting him. He'd planned every moment of their meeting, but now that she was in his arms, all he wanted to do was keep kissing her until they both went up in flames. Her hair was as dark as the night sky, soft and cool against his skin as he wrapped it around his fingers and tugged her head back. She barely came to his shoulder, so he had to lean down to kiss her properly. He wanted to crush her soft body against his, but she was still holding her daughter, and he wouldn't risk injuring Melody, not even in the thrall of the Scorching. The Gods had given him two females to protect, and he would die before he failed either of them again.

"We have to stop." Aria tore her mouth from his and pushed back, putting unwanted distance between them.

He knew she was right, but that didn't make it any easier to let her go. It was already getting difficult to think logically, and it would only get worse as the Scorching grew stronger. Flames. He needed to explain that to her as well. While the human females were aware of the Spark, they had only been told that they would be leaving with their new mates for a few Earth days to get to know each other. Even the human females already on Pyros agreed it was necessary to keep the truth about the mating fever a secret until after the Gathering. There was too much at stake to risk any misunderstandings or outright lies by those who opposed the Pyrosian claiming human females for their own.

He finally released her, though he stole another brief kiss before letting go of her hair. "I need to find a way to communicate with my people. Do you have one of the cell phone devices?"

She groaned and bowed her head. "I am so stupid. I totally forgot about it. The damned thing even has a flashlight."

He hated hearing her disparage herself. Of all the females present, she was the only one he'd seen who hadn't panicked. He caught her chin in one hand and coaxed her head up so she was looking at him. "You are not stupid. I do not like to hear you use such words to describe yourself. I've read your profile. You are an educated, intelligent woman. Your clear thinking is why you're safe in here instead of out there with the others, risking injury or worse."

She scoffed and moved her head away from his hand. "I got myself trapped with no way to contact anyone for help. There's no way my phone is going to work in here. If you hadn't come after me…"

"Whatever the attack was about, it's over now. There hasn't been an explosion since I teleported. We would have heard or felt it. They'll be looking for survivors now. Someone would have found you eventually." He held out his hand. "You got yourself and Melody to safety. And if you're willing to sacrifice your phone to the cause, I believe I can use the power supply to boost my communicator's signal.

"It's in my purse, Which is pinned under the bag for Melody's things." She tried to reach it, but the sling and her daughter were in the way.

He should have taken the bags for her, but instead he handed Aria the lightstone he'd brought with him and lifted Melody out of the sling. He cradled the baby in his arms and stared down at her in amazement. She was his to protect. His family. His future. He touched the cap of dark hair, marveling at its softness. She reached for him, grabbing his finger again, her tiny hand dwarfed by his. Without really realizing it, he lapsed into his own language. "You are as beautiful as your mother, and just as precious. I will watch over you all of your life and raise you as if you were my own."

Aria watched carefully until she was sure Melody was alright, then she got the bags untangled and pulled out her phone. "Here." She offered it to him. "I'll take Melody again."

He wasn't ready to let go of her yet, but he had to. He needed to let someone know where they were, and to do that, he needed both hands and a place to work. He returned Melody to her mother, scooped both her bags off the ground, and looked around. "We need to find somewhere more comfortable for us to wait."

Aria raised the lightstone and looked around them. "There's a door over here." He moved to her side and they approached the door together.

"Whitecaps?" He asked. While he'd learned to speak English fluently, he had not yet mastered reading the language.

"It's our soccer team. The Whitecaps. This is the door to their dressing room. There should be a place to sit down and maybe even some water in here." She started to push the door open, but he stopped her with a touch of his hand.

"I'll go in first. I know it is unlikely anyone is inside, but I need to be sure before you enter."

"You think we could still be in danger? You said the attack was over."

"I believe it is over. I am still going in first." He set down her bags and took the lightstone from her.

Her brows rose. "Anyone ever mention you're bossy?"

"I am a high-ranking officer in the Royal Guard. Giving orders is part of my job. So is safeguarding those in my care."

"I'm not in your care, though. And as nice as our kiss was, I'm not really *yours*. Once we're out of this mess, you and I need to talk."

Her words cut him to the core. He pointed to her and Melody, then thumped his hand to his chest. "You are mine, Aria Frasier. The Spark proves it. We will talk soon, but nothing you say is going to change the fact we're destined to spend our lives together."

He shoved open the door and stalked inside, almost hoping there was some threat beyond the door. That way, he could demonstrate his prowess as a warrior, and her protector. His initial plans had been reduced to rubble, but that didn't change anything. He was a soldier. He always had contingency plans. They were together now, and he would make this work. He would simply have to find another way to show Aria he was worthy of her.

EVERY TIME she thought she had figured out what kind of man Tarjen was, he showed her another facet of himself. He was brave, certainly. And when those big hands of his had gently lifted Melody out of the sling with such care and tenderness, it made her heart ache. *That* was the kind of man Melody deserved to have in her life. Too bad he was also stubborn as hell. His insistence that they were destined to be together was rankling, and the way he took charge of everything was – *hot*. Wait. No. It was annoying. Not hot at all. The same voice laughed at her from the back of her mind. *Liar*.

Great. Now she was arguing with herself.

While she'd been distracted with her inner dialogue, Tarjen had entered the locker room. She moved to the doorway, not wanting to be left alone in the darkening hallway. It felt like an eon had passed before he walked back towards her.

"It's safe, and I found a place we can be comfortable." He gestured her inside and then moved past her to gather up her bags. When he returned, he placed a gentle hand on her back and guided her inside.

His touch was like a brand searing her skin. She gasped softly, almost stumbling as an answering heat blossomed inside of her, filling her veins with fire. He caught her and drew her back against the solid bulk of his body to steady her, triggering a maelstrom of needs and wants that threatened to consume her.

"Are you well?" he asked, one hand on her hip and the other wrapped around her and Melody.

Hell no, she wasn't well. She was losing her damned mind. Why else would she turn into a gooey puddle of hormones every time Tarjen touched her? "I'm fine. You just uh, startled me. Your hand is really warm."

He frowned. "When I touched you, did you feel heat? Heat that went past the point of contact?"

"Uh, yeah." That was an understatement and a half, but she wasn't about to admit the truth.

"That is…concerning. I had hoped we would have more time before the effects of the Scorching began."

"Whoa. What effects? And what the hell is the Scorching? There was nothing in the information your people sent about any of this." She pulled out of his embrace and turned to face him, her heart pounding against her ribs. What was he talking about?

"I think you will want to sit for this conversation." He raised the light source so it illuminated the room. The walls were all fitted with identical alcoves and shelves of polished wood, each marked with a player's number and a photo of that player. There were hooks for uniforms, and chairs set in front of each locker for the players to use as they dressed.

She started towards one of the chairs, but Tarjen shook his head and pointed. "This way."

"You speak English very well, but you don't seem to be familiar with a few words - like please."

He glanced down at her, his lips curving into a brain-meltingly sexy smile. "Please, *seska*. There are more comfortable furnishings in the other room."

She couldn't help but smile back. "Thank you. I'm sure Melody would be happy to be out of her sling, too. That's the second time you've called me *seska*. What does it mean?"

"It is a term of endearment in my language. In your language, it would be similar to calling someone the beloved of my heart."

She didn't respond to that. They'd barely met. How could she be his beloved anything? He led them through a short hallway to a lounge area. There were chairs and couches scattered around the room, as well as a few tables and a water cooler.

She sank down onto one of the couches with a tired sigh and lifted Melody out of the sling. The moment she set Melody down on the couch, she started exploring. "Tarjen, can you please raise the light up so I can make sure it's safe for Melody if I put her on the floor?"

"Of course. What dangers are we looking for?"

She got back to her feet, picked up Melody, and walked around the room. "Electrical outlets, sharp objects and anything small enough for her to put in her mouth."

"Why would she eat something that might harm her?"

"Because babies put everything in their mouths. It's how they learn about things. Taste, texture, temperature. As a mother, it's terrifying, but that's how she learns."

Satisfied there was nothing in the immediate area to worry about, she placed Melody on the floor and finally got to sit down. The fear and adrenaline were fading now, leaving her weary and uncertain.

Tarjen pulled one of the chairs in close and seated himself so they're knees were almost touching. "The only small child I have ever spent time with is Hope. She is the daughter of my commander, Kash, and his mate, Gwen. Gwen is from Earth, too. I am not sure, but I believe her daughter is only a little younger than Melody."

"Gwen? You mean the spokeswoman for the Star-Crossed Dating Agency? You *know* her?" Aria reached down to help Melody get to her feet. She clung to Aria's skirt, chortling happily to herself as she fought to stay standing.

"As one of the prince's guards, I have met all the human females that currently live on Pyros, but I consider, Gwen, Princess Maggie, and Lisa to be friends. They are all from Vancouver, and they are eager to meet you and help you adjust to life on Pyros. Gwen will be pleased to have a playmate for Hope living at the palace."

Aria's thought process derailed and crashed. "The *palace*? You live in a palace? And you still haven't told me what the Scorching is. And why do you call me *seska* when we've barely met? I have a hundred or so questions, and we still need to talk about the fact that I can't go with you. This…us… it can't work."

Tarjen's brow creased and he shook his head. "It will work. It has to. We are bound together for the rest of our lives, Aria Frasier. There is no way to undo what has been done."

Aria reached down to grip her daughter's hand. "And what, *exactly*, has been done?"

"We are bonded. You witnessed the Spark. It is a sign that we are destined for each other." He paused, his dark eyes full of regret. "It also heralds the beginning of the Scorching, a mating fever that will consume us both for the next two of your days. That is what you are feeling right now." He touched one hand to his chest, his voice lowering to a low rumble. "And so am I."

CHAPTER FOUR

ARIA'S PANICKED expression tore at his heart. She was his true mate, yet she was looking at him as if he were a threat to her and her daughter instead of their protector.

"There has to be a way to undo this Spark thing. We barely know each other!" Aria's blue eyes narrowed. "And why didn't the information packet mention the Scorching? That's a hell of an omission! What else aren't you telling me?"

"There is no reversing the Spark. We believe it is the will of the Gods and welcome the moment we discover our mate. As for the choice not to mention the Scorching, that decision was made by King Janus and his advisors. They thought the females of your world would misunderstand and refuse to sign up if they thought they might be forced to do something against their will."

"They'd be right about that!"

Sensing her mother's distress, Melody screwed up

her tiny face and began to wail. Without thinking, Tarjen reached down and lifted the crying child into his arms, rocking her the way his mother had once rocked himself and his brothers. "Hush, little star, no need for tears."

Aria kept hold of Melody's hand and tried to draw her away from him. "Give her to me. She doesn't like strangers. You're going to make it worse."

Despite her mother's warning, Melody quieted, settling into his arms with an acceptance that warmed his heart. Now if only her mother would trust him the way her daughter did...

Some of the anger in Aria's eyes faded as she watched her little girl's reaction to him. "She doesn't usually do that."

"Perhaps she can sense that there is a bond between us, even if you aren't ready to, yet."

A very different kind of spark gleamed in her gaze as she locked eyes with him. "You still haven't finished explaining everything. I'm not even discussing bonds or the future until I know what the hell is going on. I want answers, and I want to get out of here so I can find my sister and my friend."

Tarjen set the lightstone down on the floor and reached for Aria's hand. She didn't offer it, but she didn't withdraw when he placed his hand over hers. "We are destined for each other, *seska*. You were told that you'd be coming with me for a few of your days to get to know each other, yes?"

"Yes. But that's hardly the same thing." She drew a

long breath, her hand tensing beneath his. "And I wasn't going to go with you, anyway."

Her words stunned him. "You weren't? Then why did you accept the match? Why come at all?"

She bit her lip and sighed. "It was an accident. I didn't see the email until my sister told me about her invitation to this event. She wasn't matched, but she was in the database and got invited. I thought I'd cancelled my profile. Then I saw the email and I was so nervous I pushed the wrong part of the screen. I didn't plan any of this, but once I'd done it, I couldn't find a way to reverse my choice. This was all a mistake, Tarjen."

"The Gods don't make mistakes." He stopped the protest he knew was coming by sealing her lips with a kiss.

The Scorching swept through him, burning away every thought in his head save one: he needed more. More kisses. More touching. More of *her*. Nothing else mattered. He eased himself to the floor, carefully setting Melody down beside him before taking hold of Aria and pulling her into his lap. As her soft weight settled on his thighs he uttered a low groan. This was what he craved more than the air he breathed. Her. Aria. His true mate.

He threaded his fingers into her hair, drawing her in close enough to kiss again. This time, she came willingly, her arms wrapping around his neck as she pressed in close and opened her mouth to him. He accepted her invitation and took the kiss deeper, his tongue dancing with hers. He allowed himself to give in to the temptation to touch her, exploring her soft, welcoming body. He palmed one of her breasts and she uttered a low, needy moan, arching herself against his hand. She was as lost as he was, both consumed by the Scorching.

"Ma-ma-ma," A child's voice cut through the lust that fogged his mind, dragging him back to reality. Guilt and shame crashed over him in an icy wave that doused the fires of the Scorching, allowing him to think clearly. He had failed them, again. Aria and her daughter were his to protect, and yet, instead of working to get them free, he'd given in to the mating fever. *I don't deserve them.*

He tore his mouth from Aria's and straightened, putting as much distance as he could between them. Not an easy thing to do when his mate was nestled in his lap. He needed to regain control and remember the plan, and the promises, he had made. He had to keep them safe.

Aria looked up at him with a wounded expression, her eyes full of confusion and hurt one second, then carefully shuttered and blank the next. She turned from him to reach for Melody, drawing the little girl into her arms.

Without a word, she scrambled out of his arms and away, never easing her hold on her daughter. Once she was seated on the furniture again, she buried her face in Melody's cap of soft hair and crooned, "Mommy's here, little one. I've got you."

"I will make the adjustments needed to boost the signal on my communicator and make contact with the *Firebrand*. We'll be out of here soon. You have my word."

Aria murmured something that sounded like an agreement, but she didn't look at him. She was withdrawing. No doubt questioning his ability to protect her the way a mate should. Given how he had been acting, she was right to worry. She deserved so much better.

Once they were safely onboard the *Firebrand*, he would do whatever it took to prove to her that he was worthy of the gift the Gods had bestowed upon him - his beautiful Aria, and her daughter.

SHE'D FORGOTTEN ABOUT MELODY. What kind of mother fell into a man's arms and completely forgot about her baby? No, she hadn't even been in the arms of a man. She'd been making out with an *alien*. Guilt curdled in her stomach, but even that wasn't enough to cool the fires raging inside her. She still wanted him. Hell, she was literally aching for him to touch her again. Not that it seemed likely he would. Since breaking off their kiss and pulling away, he hadn't even looked at her. So much for being his true mate. Once he'd gotten a feel for the extra weight she'd tried to hide under her dress, he'd pulled away.

Why had she let Haley and Piper talk her into this?

It was crazy and pointless. Once she knew her sister was safe, she was going to kill her. She closed her eyes and squeezed Melody tight. Please, oh please, let Piper and Haley be safe. If something had happened to them…

Melody squirmed in her arms and started wailing in protest.

"Sorry, baby. Am I squishing you?" She reluctantly eased her hold on her daughter, but Melody didn't want to be held. She continued to wriggle and kick, her cries getting louder. It didn't take long for Aria to recognize the problem. "You need a fresh diaper and a nap, don't you?"

The familiar task of changing a diaper helped her recover from the day's ongoing insanity. By the time she had Melody tucked into a makeshift bed, Aria was herself again, or at least as close a proximation as she could manage. Taking a seat on the couch right next to Melody, she started to hum a favourite lullaby, hoping to get her daughter to sleep for at least a little while.

Tarjen was still sitting on the floor, the lightstone giving off enough light for him to work. He had her phone in pieces on the floor, along with what must be his communicator. He had a small gadget that looked a little like a Swiss Army knife and was using it to do…*something* to her phone's battery.

"You sing beautifully," he said in soft tones.

She shook her head, embarrassed. "No, I don't. My mother had a beautiful voice. She was a classically trained soprano. Neither Piper nor I inherited her gift."

His brows furrowed as he fixed her with an intense look. "I like the way you sing. Your voice is pretty, and I could hear how much your daughter means to you. Your heart was in the notes."

Her heart did a triple-flip in her chest, but she shut down her body's traitorous reactions before she lost control again. She cemented her resolve by reminding them both where her priorities lay. "Melody is the most important thing in my life. I'd die to protect her, and I will do everything in my power to give her the best life I can."

"You are her protector," he mused, nodding. "As I am both of yours."

"I want more for Melody than just a protector."

He raised his gaze to hers, and once again she had to fight the urge to throw herself off the couch and back into his arms. "What else do you want, *seska*?"

That was the billion-dollar question. She raised her hands in a gesture of confusion. "I don't know. I, well, I know I want someone kind. And faithful. That's a must."

He nodded, listening without interrupting her as he continued to tinker with the communicator.

"And?" he prompted when she didn't say anything more.

"And someone who will love Melody unconditionally, even though she isn't his by blood." She hesitated, then added. "And my sister thinks I deserve someone who wants to take care of me and will make me the center of their universe."

When she was finished, he raised the communicator in triumph. "It will work now. As soon as I have contacted the *Firebrand*, I will address what you have said."

She wanted to scream. Every time they seemed to be making some kind of progress, he withdrew. How the hell was this going to work if they couldn't even have a simple conversation? Not that she was expecting it to work. In fact, there was no it. No them. No chance. *And if I keep repeating that, maybe my hormones will come out of hyperdrive.*

He got to his feet, picking up the lightstone and placing it in her hands before leaning down to press a gentle kiss to her forehead. "I heard all you said, and I wish to answer, but my first duty is to protect you both and get you to safety."

"Thank you for explaining."

"I am not used to explaining myself to others. The only ones I answer to are the royal family and my commander, Kash." He sighed. "I did not take that into consideration when I prepared for this meeting. I will strive to do better."

"You prepared for this? For meeting me? How?"

He smiled and stroked her cheek, and for a second his eyes seemed to gleam gold in the dim light. "I will explain once I have made contact. And once we are back on board, I will be able to show you, too."

He moved to the far side of the room and tapped something on the side of the device. It lit up and he grinned at her, then started speaking words she couldn't begin to understand. His tone sharpened, and each syllable crackled and snapped as he spoke. Another male voice answered in what seemed to be the same language, and after a few short minutes, he shut off the communicator. The only words she recognized in the entire conversation were her name, Melody, Haley, and Piper.

He settled onto the couch beside her and turned to face her. "Help is coming. My people have our location and will bring equipment to clear the rubble and make a path for us."

"That's good news. I don't suppose you have any news on my sister or my friend? I heard you mention their names."

"I'm sorry, there was no information on either of them. The wounded of both species were taken to our ships to be treated, and things are still chaotic. I can tell you that no female humans were killed in the attack. Wherever your companions are, they are alive."

She breathed a sigh of relief and the knot in her chest loosened a little. "Thank you." Then the rest of what he said sank in. "Wait. You said no female humans. What about males? What about your species?"

"The area where the mayor and other high-ranking guests were seated was not targeted, but several security officers and organizers were killed in the explosions." His mouth turned down at the corners. "As were many of my fellow Pyrosians. They came to claim their matches and start a new chapter in their lives, and now they're dead. It's hard to accept."

"I'm sorry, Tarjen. This was not the way you should have been welcomed to our world." She went against everything in her training and reached for his hand, covering it with hers. He turned his hand and gripped hers tight.

"You are not to blame for the actions of others. You have nothing to apologize for."

"I know, but it's a human thing. We say we're sorry when we sense someone is hurting. Did you know any of the males killed?"

He shook his head. "I don't think so. There were five hundred or so of us claiming mates at this event, but because of my job, I travelled with the Prince and didn't spend much time with the others."

"And the Prince and Princess are alright? I thought I saw their shuttle flying away after the explosions started."

"They are unhurt, as is my commander, his mate, and their daughter." He lifted her hand to his mouth and feathered several soft kisses over her knuckles. "Soon, everyone that I care for will be safely onboard the *Firebrand*."

"And then what?"

The look he gave her was hot enough to weld steel. "Then we let the Scorching take us. By then, both of us will be too far gone to control ourselves."

"What about Melody? I'm not leaving my little girl to get naked with you!" She tried to pull her hand back, but he didn't let go. After a few seconds of tugging, she gave up with a disgruntled huff and glared at him.

He chuckled, and somehow it made him even sexier. Her pulse raced and her fingers tingled everywhere he'd kissed her. "I will ask Gwen if she would watch over Melody for you. That way our daughter would be in the nursery, close by. You will be able to see her during the lulls when the Scorching fades for a time. She will be guarded and cared for like the treasure that she is."

"Wait. Did you just call her *our* daughter?" For the second time in an hour, she found herself in Tarjen's lap. He lifted her as if she weighed nothing at all, then wrapped his arms around her and gave her a sweet and sexy smile that made her brain melt around the edges.

"I did. That is how I think of her. She is a precious gift." He bowed his head to nuzzle her lips. "As are you. Come with me, and I promise that you will be the star I orbit for the rest of our lives. There will be no one else for me, *seska*. Once we complete the bond, I will never desire another female as long as I live."

"This is crazy."

He cupped her cheek in his hand and stared into her eyes. "For you, it must feel this way. For me, there is nothing crazy about it. This is what was meant to be."

Need coursed through her, accompanied by an even more intoxicating feeling: hope. Her resolve shattered like glass striking concrete as she let go of her fear and kissed him. The moment her lips touched his, the fire in her blood became an inferno.

His fingers tangled in her hair, supporting her head as he took control of the kiss. She moaned into his mouth, her hands exploring every part of him she could reach. He cupped her breast, rubbing his thumb over her already taut nipple, and she squirmed as her clit started to pulse and her pussy grew slicker with every touch. She was sitting across his lap with the impressive ridge of his rock-hard cock pressing into her hip.

Breathless and giddy, she felt like all her senses were dialed up to eleven. She craved his touch, the subtle, spicy musk of his scent, even the taste of his mouth as he kissed her. "Too much," she muttered, barely aware she was speaking. "Hurts."

"It's the Scorching. We're running out of time." He nipped her lower lip and slid one big hand down her legs, not stopping until he hit bare skin. "Let me ease your pain."

"How?"

"If you reach orgasm, the need will subside for a little while."

Embarrassed, she closed her eyes and nodded once. "Afterward, I can help you the same way?"

He uttered a rueful chuckle. "As much as I want your hands on me right now, it wouldn't do any good. There will be no reprieve for me until we are fully mated. I have waited my entire life to find true release, I can wait a little longer."

"What?" he couldn't mean what she thought he did. Could he? It had to be a translation error.

"Pyrosian males only reach orgasm with their destined mate." He gave her a lopsided grin. "I'm looking forward to finding out what that feels like."

"Never? Oh wow. I hope you're not disappointed…"

He didn't answer her in words, but his next kiss was so hot she almost came on the spot. When he stroked his fingers up the inside of her thigh, she parted her legs for him and uttered a moan so loud she worried she'd wake Melody. When his fingers reached the silken crotch of her panties, Aria had to bite back another moan. Her toes curled and her whole body tensed in anticipation of what came next.

CHAPTER FIVE

TARJEN KNEW they didn't have long before the others arrived, but he would make the time they had left count. Then he would bring his new family to the Firebrand, see to it Melody was safe, and spend the next few days proving to Aria that he could be everything she wanted in a mate.

Her soft moans vibrated against his tongue as he kissed her, and when his fingers brushed over the delicate fabric covering her pussy he uttered a low groan of his own when he discovered she was already wet and ready for him. He moved the cloth aside and slid a digit inside her desire-slicked folds. She bucked her hips against his hand, grinding herself against him. Her passionate response made his cock so hard he could have punched through the hull of a battlecruiser with it. He couldn't wait to lay claim to her lush body and complete their mating. She was so much more than the fantasy he'd clung to all these years. Her file had told him the facts of her life but meeting her – flames and fury – she was amazing.

It didn't take long for him to find the delicate bundle of nerves he'd read about in his research. He circled it with one finger, then gently stroked over the area. Her response was breathtaking. A soft intake of breath, a thrust of her hips, her toes curled with pleasure.

"Yes?" he broke off their kiss to ask.

She laughed and peeked up at him. "So much yes."

"As you wish," he replied.

She laughed even harder. "*The Princess Bride*? How do you know about that movie?"

"I did my research." He stroked his fingers over her clit again, using more pressure this time. She moaned, wrapped her arms around his neck and whispered, "I can see that. Don't stop." Then she kissed him again, and his world went up in flames.

He followed her request to the letter, providing her with unrelenting pleasure every way he could think of. He fingered her clit hard and fast, working her into a frenzy. She rode his fingers eagerly, and when he changed positions and slid two fingers into her tight channel, her wordless keening cry told him she was close. He pressed the pad of his thumb against her clit as he fucked her with his hand, watching as she finally lost control and came apart in his arms.

When the moment passed, she sagged against him, breathless and spent. He raised his head, lingering to brush a soft kiss to the corner of her mouth. Her eyes fluttered open and she gifted him with a shy smile.

"Better?" he asked.

She gave a slight nod, her smile widening. "Much. I can think clearly again."

He withdrew his hand from her body, placing those same fingers in his mouth so he could savour the taste of her. "You are delectable."

She blushed. "If you say so."

"I do. And I will keep saying it until you believe me." His communicator chimed several times in succession, and he knew their time was up. He should have warned her, but instead he smoothed her dress back over her legs and kissed her again. He wasn't ready to let her go.

There was a low hum, the air in the room shifted, and they were no longer alone. Six members of the royal guard appeared about ten feet away, at the precise coordinates he'd provided.

"Senior Guardsman Rix. We're here to escort you and your family to safety, sir."

The Scorching was affecting him so badly it took a moment for him to remember the young male's name. "Guardsman Dres, what are you doing here? You and your men should be guarding the prince."

A familiar chuckle from the shadows filled the room. "Did you really think the prince was going to send some random member of the ship's crew to retrieve you and your mate? We're here at his order. The threat's down here, not on board the *Firebrand*." Keth, one of his oldest friends, stepped into the circle of light and grinned. "It's good to see you alive and well. We've been worried."

Aria looked at the new arrivals, then skewered him with a look he was already starting to recognize. She was annoyed with him…again. "You might have warned me we were about to have company."

"They were quicker getting here then I expected."

"You mean you decided to kiss me instead of telling me they were on their way."

"If I had a female as lovely as you in my arms, I would have made the same choice." Keth stepped forward and offered her his hand, human-fashion. "I'm Keth, a member of the Royal Guard, and a friend of your mate's. It's good to meet you, Aria of Earth."

"It's nice to meet you, too." Aria took Keth's hand and used it to extract herself from Tarjen's lap.

Seeing her touch another male had him on his feet a second later, one arm wrapping possessively around her waist as he drew her away from his best friend. The other guards vanished into the shadows, no doubt to start clearing the rubble.

"Tarjen!" Aria twisted her head around to glare at him. "No grabbing."

"Apologies, *seska*. It is getting difficult to think."

Keth merely took another step back. "It's progressing quickly, then?"

"Very. We need to get back to the ship as soon as possible." The Scorching was consuming him, shredding his control and making it harder to focus with every passing second.

"You could teleport back to the ship immediately. I will bring the child by shuttle."

"No." Both he and Aria spoke at the same time.

Keth grinned. "It seems you are already in agreement on some things, at least. We'll clear the rubble as quickly as possible. You'll all be back on board the ship soon. This planet seems to get more dangerous each time we visit. I'll be happy once all of our people, and their mates, are safely in orbit and away from this place."

Aria tensed, and Tarjen shot his friend a warning look over the top of her head. Anyone who upset his mate would pay a steep price, even his life-long friend.

Keth quickly changed the subject. "The equipment we use will make a significant amount of noise. Perhaps you should wake your daughter, so she is not startled?"

"Good idea." Aria wriggled in his arms. "Let me go so I can see to Melody."

He released her, but followed, keeping himself between his family and Keth. He couldn't help himself. This was one of the reasons why newly mated couples were isolated during the time of the Scorching. It lessened the odds of fights breaking out if someone stood too close to another's mate.

"How bad is it?" Aria asked, her voice pitched low enough only he could hear her.

"I will survive."

She rolled her eyes. "Of course you will, no one ever died of a lack of nookie."

He didn't recognize the word she used, but he worked out her meaning. "Actually… we can."

"Well, shit. Don't do that, okay?" She gave him a worried smile, and then turned to lift Melody. Without hesitating, she turned back and offered him the still sleepy child. "Here, if you hold her, I can pack up her blanket and things. That way, we'll be ready to go as soon as they clear a path."

He settled the baby against his shoulder. She snuggled into his arms, uttering a tiny sigh, and all the pieces of his life fell into place with perfect clarity and a sense of abiding calm that held even the Scorching at bay…for now.

Keth went to join the others, and Tarjen didn't see him again until the way had been cleared and they were escorted to a waiting shuttlecraft. As he helped Aria aboard, Keth came running out of the stadium, holding an unconscious female in his arms. Her blonde hair fell across her face in bloody tangles, and it wasn't until Keth got her inside that Tarjen recognized the female as the same one who had been assigned to his group, the one who had learned enough of their language to wish them good luck.

"Eva!" Aria gasped and leaned against her safety harness to get a better look at the female Keth was carefully securing into place on one of the bench-style seats that lined the walls of the shuttle.

"Is that her name?" Keth glanced over at Aria, then back to Eva. "It is as beautiful as she is."

Understanding dawned. "She is your mate?" Tarjen asked in Pyrosian.

Keth nodded, his gaze still locked on Eva. "I found her trapped in the rubble. When I touched her hand, I saw the Spark fly between us." He buckled in beside her, his hand on her brow, slowing the bleeding from the gash on her head. "Torel will save her. He has to."

"What are you saying? Is she going to be okay?" Aria interjected.

Tarjen switched to English. "Keth found her trapped in the rubble. We'll get her to the ship for treatment."

"Why don't you just teleport there? Wouldn't it be faster?"

Keth answered first. "She has a head injury. It isn't safe."

She wrinkled her nose. "So, teleportation is not safe for children or anyone with injuries. Why do you use it at all if it's so unsafe?"

"Because when sneaking around a strange new world that doesn't know aliens exist, it's best to be subtle," Tarjen explained.

"Subtle, huh? I don't think that word means what you think it means."

He recognized the movie quote and even caught the meaning behind it. He was finally getting familiar with the slang and cultural references of Aria's part of the world. Soon, he'd understand everything he needed to about Aria and once he did, everything between them would be perfect. It was only a matter of time.

THE SHUTTLE RIDE was almost over before she realized they had taken off. She had expected a rocket-launch style rumble, or at the very least the sudden acceleration of a jet taxing down a runway. There was nothing like that. It wasn't until Tarjen activated a viewscreen and showed her a real-time image of the planet spinning slowly beneath them that she grasped the reality of her situation. She wasn't on Earth anymore. She was in space, on her way to an alien vessel with a man she barely knew. Panic dug its sharp claws into her chest, but as quickly as it struck, it vanished as Tarjen reached over and squeezed her hand.

"Your world is beautiful."

"We're going back, right?"

He nodded. "Once the Scorching passes, we'll return. You will see your sister and friend again."

Piper. Why hadn't anyone heard from her or Haley? Where were they? "I'm worried about them. I know we're going to be distracted soon, but please, if anyone hears from my sister or my friend, I need to know. I'm worried. Other than Melody, they're the only family I have left."

"I will see to it," Tarjen promised.

They lapsed into silence after that. She watched Keth tend to Eva, amazed at the tenderness and affection he showed the woman despite the fact they'd never so much as spoken. "Is she his mate?"

"She is." Keth answered without looking up. "I only pray that she is not taken from me before we have even begun our life together."

Aria didn't know what to say. Everything she thought of sounded trite. "I hope so, too," she finally said. There had been enough death and sadness today.

The ship touched down with a gentle thud, and she glanced at Tarjen. "What did we land on?"

"The floor of the shuttle bay. It's a large hangar, full of ships and people." The charming smile of earlier was gone, now. It had to be the effects of the Scorching.

"So, we can breathe? What about gravity?" She wished she had thought to ask these questions earlier, but, kissing him had seemed like a much better use of her time.

"Atmosphere and gravity are much like they are on your world. You'll see."

They stayed seated as Keth carried Eva out a doorway that simply appeared in a bulkhead near the front of the ship. One minute there was nothing and the next, *poof*. Door. Beyond was an empty white room, but before she could get a good look, the door closed with Keth, Eva, and the shuttle pilot inside.

"That's the shuttle bay?"

"That's the airlock. It's also a decontamination chamber. It takes a few minutes to cycle. Once they're on their way to medical, we'll go in. Be ready." His hand tightened around hers and he exhaled sharply.

"It's getting worse, isn't it?" she hated knowing he was suffering, but she didn't know how to help him.

Coping with grief after her mother's death had led her to the field of psychology, but nothing in her training prepared her for this. His pain was her fault, at least in part, and she wanted to do something, anything, to make it better.

"I will endure this, because when it is over I will have you and Melody."

Before she could answer, his communicator beeped. "That's Keth telling us he's left the airlock. Our turn."

"This isn't going to hurt Melody, is it?"

"I would never risk harming her. The process is safe. You won't feel a thing."

He got to his feet, then turned and released her from the unfamiliar clasps of the safety harness. It was a short walk to the spot where the door had appeared before. Tarjen waved his hand over a spot, and the wall vanished again.

The room beyond was small, brightly lit, and completely barren save for a panel set into one wall. He went over to it and tapped the screen multiple times, then returned to her side. When he took her hand again, he was warmer than he'd been only a moment ago.

"This won't take long. You'll see the lights change colours several times as part of the process. After that, it will be safe for us to leave the ship. I expect we'll be met and escorted to somewhere you can meet with Maggie, Gwen, and Lisa."

"Okay." She tightened her arms around Melody. She was expected to hand her daughter over to strangers. It didn't feel right. How could it?

"I should warn you, while everyone on board can speak a little of your language, they're not all fluent. Most of them opted to learn a small amount of several common Earth languages.

"I read about that in the pamphlet. You can learn languages quite quickly. Something about a learning program?"

"Cognitive augmentation. It's a kind of knowledge upload. It can be done while we sleep."

"Later, I want to hear more about that."

"Later," he agreed, and leaned down to kiss her. Within seconds, the Scorching had roared back to life like gasoline tossed on a campfire. Logic lost out to lust, and when he scooped her into his arms, she wrapped herself around him like a cat, Melody carefully nestled between them.

She didn't notice anything on the way to meet the others. She caught a few vague impressions of a large, open space, then a busy, brightly lit corridor and more doors that appeared and disappeared, but what little focus she had was devoted to kissing Tarjen and holding tight to her daughter.

TARJEN HAD ENDURED basic military training without breaking. He'd been injured in combat and even survived growing up the youngest of four brothers, but by the Flames of the First One, if he didn't complete his mating bond with Aria soon it might just kill him.

His cock throbbed with every heartbeat, it felt as if his blood was boiling in his veins, and every part of him ached with need. The Princess would have to forgive him, because he had no intention of staying a second longer than it took to convince Aria to leave Melody with Maggie, Gwen, and Lisa.

Their escort opened a door and stood aside with a wordless nod. Tarjen stepped through, too distracted by the Scorching to even be aware of what room he was entering. It only took a second for him to figure it out, though. There was only one place on the ship decorated in primary colours and full of toys of every shape and size. They were in the nursery.

All three females were present, and all of them were grinning as he reluctantly set Aria on her feet. Once he straightened, he managed a passable bow, and Aria copied him.

"Your Highness, ladies. I would like to present my mate, Aria Frasier and our daughter, Melody."

"Congratulations on claiming your mate." Maggie's greeting was almost drowned out by a delighted squeal as Gwen rushed toward them.

"Hi there, I'm Gwen. The preggers one is Maggie, and this is Lisa. We're so glad to meet you and your little girl." She reached out to stroke a dark finger over Melody's cheek. "She's adorable."

"Thank you. Tarjen told me that you have a little girl, too? I'm sorry, I can't remember her name. Honestly, I barely remember my name right now, it has been a hell of a day. Uh…why do you have gold eyes?"

Gwen laughed. "My eyes changed when I mated with Kash. The odds are, yours will, too. It's a Pyrosian thing. I remember what it was like when Kash and I went through the Scorching last year. It was…uh… " she trailed off, shaking her head.

"Insane? Incredible? Mind-meltingly awesome with a side of what the hell am I doing?" Lisa interjected.

"How about all of the above?" Maggie said, coming over to join them.

"That…sounds about right. But did any of you get bombed the first day you met?"

Lisa laughed. "Bombed, no. I crashed Vadir's ship though. Right in the middle of the mountains. No one could find us for a few days."

"We could have crashed?" Aria stiffened, and he wrapped his arms around her, drawing her back against his chest.

"No, *seska*. You were in no danger."

"Not unless you slugged your pilot for abducting you." Lisa agreed.

"Abducted?"

Lisa shrugged. "Vadir claims he just wanted to get me alone so he could explain everything without me running off. I still say he abducted me. It gives us something to fight about." She grinned. "Which leads to great makeup sex."

The mere mention of the word had him biting back a groan.

Gwen must have sensed his issue, because she gave him an understanding smile, then set a gentle hand on

Aria's shoulder. "I think it's time you and Tarjen were alone. Will you permit me to watch over your little girl? She'll be right here, waiting for you whenever you want to see her."

"This feels wrong."

"It isn't. This is the Scorching. There's nothing on Earth that comes close to what you're experiencing right now. You're not giving in to temptation, or lust, or being a bad mother. This is…" Gwen trailed off.

Maggie picked up where her friend left off. "This is what the Gods intended for you both. Embrace it. I hope you are as happy as the three of us are with our mates."

"Her formula and diapers and things are in the bag Tarjen's holding. It should be enough."

"I'll have the ship's computer scan some and replicate it, don't worry," Gwen told her.

Aria was trembling as she bowed her head to kiss Melody's cheek. "I'll be back soon, little one. Mommy loves you."

Gwen took the cooing baby into her arms and smiled at Aria. "She's going to be fine. I'll introduce her to Hope and I expect the next time you see her, they will have become the best of friends."

Lisa looked at Melody and then swore under her breath. "So that's why I drew that picture! I thought it was Hope and Maggie's baby together, but it's not. It was Melody I saw." The blonde beamed. "I saw them cuddled up together, sleeping. It's going to be fine, Aria.

You and your daughter are right where you're supposed to be."

"Lisa is a gifted psychic with no filters," Maggie explained. "But if she says it's going to be fine, you can trust that it will be."

"I…uh, thank you." Aria turned her head to look up at him, her eyes shimmering with tears. "There's a lot you didn't mention, Tarjen. Later, you need to fill in the gaps."

He gripped her hips and spun her around to kiss her, raising her into the air until they were eye to eye. "Later, I will tell you anything and everything you want to know. Much, much, later."

She looked over to the females. "I think this means he's done waiting."

He managed an awkward bow as the females grinned and giggled. "I think you're right. You're dismissed, Guardsman Rix," the princess released him with a wave of her hand.

"Have fun," Gwen called out.

"Don't forget to tell her about the fire thing!" Lisa added.

"Fire?" Aria asked, her question less than a whisper against his lips.

"Later." He wanted to tell her more. To explain what was about to happen, but he was out of words and out of time. He'd make it up to her, though. After all, they had the rest of their lives for him to make things right.

CHAPTER SIX

Despite what Gwen and Maggie said, Aria was wracked with guilt. She was leaving her daughter with strangers to have sex with a man she barely knew. *I am never going to win mother of the year after this.*

Not even her guilt was enough to overcome the effects of the Scorching, though. She let Tarjen carry her out of the nursery without protest, her entire body burning with need. They crossed a bright, gleaming stretch of hallway, and within seconds he had activated one of the panels that lined the walls and a door slid open.

He entered a dimly lit room, then spun around to press her up against the nearest wall. His mouth branded hers, his big body holding her in place as he tore away her clothes. Dress, bra, and panties were destroyed and cast aside. His uniform was more of a challenge for her, and eventually he lifted his head and took a step back, though his gaze never left her face.

"You have broken me, *seska*. I need you too much to take this slow."

"I don't need slow. I just need you." When he'd stepped away, she had wrapped her arms across her body, hiding as much of herself as she could. It took all the courage she had to reach for him, letting him see exactly what his Gods had chosen for him. Big hips, thick thighs, extra rolls and all. She waited for his reaction. Every man she'd ever been with had one. Would he crack a joke about there being more of her to love? Look away in silent judgement, or sigh and turn the lights off so that he wouldn't have to look at her?

The last thing she expected was for him to strip off his uniform and drop to his knees at her feet. She thought he looked huge and imposing in the dark, form-fitting garment, but naked, he looked even bigger. He took her hands in his and looked up at her with desire blazing in his eyes. For a moment, they changed from dark brown to a shimmering gold, and this time she knew what it meant - he wanted her. "You are so beautiful. I don't know what I did to deserve someone like you, Aria Frasier, but I will spend the rest of my life trying to be worthy of you and your daughter."

She couldn't believe it. This sexy, courageous man thought he wasn't worthy of *her*?

"I think you already are."

"Then I am the luckiest male in the galaxy." He placed one of her hands on his shoulder and gave her a slow, sexy grin. "You will want to hang on tight for this next part."

"To what?"

"Me." He took hold of her calf, coaxing her to lift it off the floor and then draped her leg over his other shoulder. Before she even had her balance, he leaned in and buried his face between her thighs. He parted her labia with his fingers, exposing her clit and lashing it with bold strokes of his tongue. His fingers found her entrance and pushed inside, adding new levels of pleasure. Feeling brazen, she cupped the back of his hand with one hand and pulled him closer, grinding her pussy against his mouth.

He devoured her with the fervor of a starving man, licking and sucking. His fingers curled the perfect amount as he pumped them in and out of her body. Within minutes her limbs were shaking and she was babbling a torrent of pleas. "Tarjen, yes. Like that. Please. Gods, don't stop. Yes!"

He growled her name, the sound vibrating against her clit. He drove her to the edge of her control, then pushed her off, sending her soaring on the waves of the most intense orgasm of her life. At the height of it, his teeth closed gently on her clitoris, sending her even higher and making her see stars.

Her legs turned to jelly and she started to slide down the wall. He caught her easily, lifting her with him as he rose from the floor. It took a moment to untangle themselves, but then her legs were around his hips and he had her back to the wall again. This time, the hard, pulsing length of his cock was nestled against her pussy. She was so hot, the surface of the wall felt like solid ice. She arched away from it with a gasp, rubbing her pussy over his cock.

He groaned and lifted her a few inches higher so they were perfectly positioned. She twined her arms around his neck, looked into his eyes, and nodded.

He lowered her onto his cock with care, though she could feel the toll it took on him to move so slowly. His muscles strained, and his lips were pressed into a thin line that didn't soften until he was buried hilt-deep inside her. Then he cupped her cheek in one hand and spoke. "I vow by the Flames of the First One, to protect my mate—you, Aria Frasier and your beautiful daughter, from all who would do you harm. You will be my center, my beloved, and my most cherished companion from now until we return to the Flame that birthed us."

The words were clearly a ritual, but she didn't know her part. So, instead of speaking, she simply leaned in and kissed him, hoping he understood how much his words meant. His tongue tangled with hers as he took over their kiss, initiating a dance that mimicked the slow give and take of his thrusts. Need coursed through her, and she rode his hips with a wanton eagerness she had never dared to show before.

He drove into her with relentless power, mouths mated, bodies blending together into one perfect whole. She took everything he offered, every stroke and bruising thrust, and then returned it in kind. The Scorching consumed them both, burning away everything until they existed in a perfect bubble of pleasure.

She flexed her inner walls around his cock and clung to him as he fucked her, his need for her evident in every touch and kiss. She moaned his name into the heat of his mouth, every sound she uttered driving him to greater efforts.

He came first, throwing back his head and crying out in his own language. As he thrust into her one last time, she felt his cock swell and throb inside her, stretching her inner walls and pressing against nerves she didn't know she had. It was enough to make her come again, every clench of her pussy milking his cock.

Breathless and giddy, she lowered her head to the crook of his neck, letting the subtle spice flavour of his scent surround her. It wasn't until she tasted salt that she realized there were tears on her cheeks.

Tarjen must have felt them too, because he nuzzled her hair, still breathing hard. "Did I hurt you? I'm sorry, *seska*. I didn't intend…I lost all control."

She lifted her head and smiled at him. "I know you lost control. I think that's why I'm crying. No one has ever wanted me the way you did just now. It was a little overwhelming, but in a good way."

He kissed away her tears. "I will always want you. We are one now. Bound together for the rest of our lives."

When he moved away again, she noticed something had changed. "Your eyes. They're gold. I mean, you said that would happen, but… they're really gold."

"And yours shine like gems. You are even more lovely, now, my mate, and all who look upon you will know you are claimed."

She started to squirm as she looked around the room for a mirror so she could see for herself, then froze when she realized they were still firmly locked together. "Uh, Tarjen? We're still stuck."

"That would be one of the many things I still need to explain to you. When the males of my species reach orgasm, there is a temporary swelling. It will end soon…unless you start moving again. If you do, we're going to be at it again before I even get you to the bed."

"Again? Already?" she blinked at him in shock.

He burst out laughing. "Yes, again. For the next two of your days you and I will crave each other almost constantly. There are short lulls when we can sleep, and eat, and visit Melody, but most of the time, you and I will be in the thrall of the Scorching."

"What else don't I know? Lisa mentioned flames. That sounds kind of important."

"Now we are mated, I have unlocked my ability to summon and control fire. I won't attempt it until I am calmer, and you have nothing to fear. My flames cannot hurt you."

"You can control *fire*? You guys sure left a few key details out of the brochures, didn't you?" She remembered something from the information packet she'd been sent. The reason you and I were able to mate was because I have traces of Pyrosian DNA, right? Is that why my eyes changed? Does this mean I can control fire, too? Oh god, can Melody? Is she going to get upset one day and set her crib on fire?"

"Bed first, and then I will answer your questions." He walked over to the bed, giving her a chance to look around his quarters. It wasn't what she expected.

The furnishings were done in red and gold fabrics, and the walls were a warm, buttery yellow. Everywhere she looked she saw rich fabrics and elegant furnishing. There was a small sitting area with two chairs facing each other over a table that appeared to be hand carved from some sort of black stone, and another table about the right size for two people to eat at. Both tables were covered with flowers, candles, and several boxes of her favourite chocolates. She could tell the brand by the distinct purple and gold lid. "You got me Purdy's? How do you even know about those?"

"You listed it as one of your favourite foods." He carefully withdrew from her before setting her down in the middle of the large bed that took up the center of the room.

She sank down into the sumptuous coverlet, too relaxed and contented to move. "I'm surprised you remember. No one seems to read that kind of stuff on dating sites. They just look at your picture and decide if they think you're hot."

"Courtship rituals on your planet are complicated and strange. Our way is simpler."

"Until you run out of women." She pointed out.

He stretched out beside her, his massive body curved around hers. "Some believe that the Gods did it to us on purpose to force us to explore the galaxy again, like we used to do before we grew complacent."

"Is that how I ended up with Pyrosian DNA?" It had to be, but she wanted to be sure.

"We believe so, yes. And to answer your earlier question, our ability to control fire only comes after we have found our true mates. Melody may be able to do it one day, but not until she is mated. We have many years before that happens."

"And me? I'm mated. Do you think I can?"

He was quiet for a long moment. "I don't know. The only one who has manifested that ability so far is Gwen."

"And she's the only one of the three I met who has gold eyes." She felt an odd pang of disappointment. "I guess you'll be in charge of lighting candles and the barbeque, then."

"You wish me to light the candles? They have a very pleasing scent."

"Not yet." She lifted her head to look at the myriad of gifts laid out for her. "Where did you find it all? It all looks like it's from my planet, not yours."

Her big, buff, alien bedmate blushed. "I asked Maggie to help me pick the right courtship gifts. She introduced me to online shopping. I read your file and tried to find things that would make you happy."

It was the sweetest thing anyone had ever done for her. He'd done all this, and she had barely even read his profile. She had been so convinced he'd never want her or

Melody she hadn't wanted to know anything about him. She still didn't know how this was going to work, but she was starting to realize that she would never forgive herself if she didn't give Tarjen a chance. He was everything she wanted, both for herself and her daughter.

She turned back, smiling, and found him staring at her with an expression that made her throat tighten and her heart race. It was desire, mixed with devotion and tenderness. "It's perfect, thank you."

FOR THE FIRST time since they'd met, Aria looked truly happy. Despite everything that had happened to them, they were here, together, and mated. It wasn't exactly how he'd planned things, but they had gotten there in the end.

He held her in his arms, learning the curves of her body as he explained to her some of the things there had been no time for, before. "You're telling me that the first time your race came here, the women had no idea you were aliens? Maggie, Lisa? None of them knew? You just came along and took them?"

"You have to understand, we were desperate. According to the laws of the Inter-Planetary Council, we weren't even supposed to be in this part of the galaxy, and first contact is only supposed to be made with species that have reached certain milestones. Milestones that your species are still generations away from achieving. Even then, we never intended to abduct the females outright."

"Then why did Lisa say she was kidnapped?"

He opted for the more diplomatic reply. "Because in some cases, things did not proceed as planned."

"Apparently." She said, her tone as dry as dust. "So, there were *unplanned* abductions?"

He chuckled at her question. "There were. Joran slipped away from his escort and went to meet Maggie ahead of schedule. Until they met, we had no idea if the Spark would manifest between our races. When it did, he had to adapt, quickly. Vadir had much the same issue. They both chose to teleport their mates away without permission, but in the end, their mates forgave them."

"I bet that didn't happen right away."

He recalled the first time he met Maggie and chuckled again. "It did not. I was one of the guardsmen Joran ditched to meet Maggie, and I was there as the two of them worked things out. I'm glad they did. She has made Joran a very happy male and ensured that one day, he will take the throne."

"They made the decision to stay after the Scorching had stopped messing with their minds, right?"

He bristled. "Of course we waited until their minds were clear. We are an honourable race. Far more advanced and civilized than humans. When you come with me to Pyros, you will see for yourself."

"Did you just call my entire species uncivilized?

We're far from perfect, but from what you just told me, you Pyrosians aren't, either."

"No, we aren't. But we are advanced enough not to go around blowing up innocent people and attacking allies," he pointed out. "Your sister and friend are missing because of humans, not Pyrosians."

Regret hit milliseconds after he spoke, but by then it was too late. Aria sat up, her arms folding over her chest, her body stiff. "You're right. Humans tend to fear what we don't understand. However, it's become apparent that the Pyrosians haven't exactly been upfront about things, so maybe we're right to be fearful of you." She thumped her chest. "I should be back on Earth, looking for the people I care about, but because of this stupid Scorching thing, I've barely thought about Piper. You should have told us! The governments would never have agreed to this if they'd known what this whole Star-Crossed Dating idea actually entailed!"

"They knew, *seska*. They knew, and they all agreed it would be best if certain facts weren't made known to the general public right away."

She narrowed her eyes and fixed him with a stare that made him feel like a youngling again. "And how's that plan working out for you so far? Your prince nearly got blown up today. Do you think that's a coincidence?"

Her words reminded him of his failures. She wasn't the only one whose mind had been addled by the mating fever. It was his sworn duty to protect the prince and princess, and he had allowed himself to be distracted by the prospect of meeting his mate. His distraction had put everyone he was supposed to protect at risk.

"Tarjen?" Her soft voice spoke his name, but it was her touch that drew him out of his dark thoughts. "What's wrong? One minute we were arguing and then you went totally silent. Like you weren't even in the room."

"You aren't the only one whose mind has been affected by the Scorching," he said, evading her question. He didn't want to remind her of his failings. Not now, when his plans were finally coming together. From now on, things would proceed as he had intended.

She made a non-committal noise in the back of her throat, but her hand glided down his forearm to cover his hand. "I think maybe we should try that chocolate now."

"And light the candles?" he asked, rising from the bed.

"Yes, please. Then could you turn down the lights? I'm not used to lounging around naked without the lights being dimmed, or off."

"Off? If the lights were out, how would I see you?"

She blushed and drew part of the bed covers across her lower body. "You wouldn't."

"Then the lights stay on."

"You want to see me?"

Anger boiled inside him. Someone had convinced his mate she wasn't beautiful. He hadn't been there to protect her from those lies, but he would spend the rest of his life proving to her that it wasn't true.

Still angry, he reached for the chocolates she had requested, then froze and stared at his hand. It was engulfed in flames. *I summoned fire!*

Grinning, he held up his hand and turned to show Aria. "My ability has manifested."

Her eyes widened, and she watched in silence, transfixed by the flames. "I guess lighting those candles won't be a problem now, huh?"

He pointed his finger at the nearest candle, willing it to catch fire. For several long seconds, nothing happened, but then a portion of the flame arced from his hand to the candle wick, setting it ablaze. After that, it was a matter of moments to light the other candles and then banish the flames that still burned around his hand. Elated and proud, he selected one of the larger boxes of candy he'd procured for Aria and returned to their bed.

He handed her the box, stacked the pillows against the headboard, then coaxed her to join him, arms outstretched in invitation. "Come, *seska*. We won't have long until the mating fever returns, and I know you have more questions. Plus, I would like to try these chocolates you enjoy."

She moved up beside him, and he was pleased to note she allowed the sheets to fall away, baring her lower body again. "You've never had chocolate?"

"I do not believe so. Vadir has imported small amounts of human food, but most of it went to the human females already on Pyros, and the rest was served to the royal family and their court as a curiosity. I do like waffles, though. And coffee. Before we leave, I hope to be able to sample both again."

"I think I can arrange that. My sister makes the best waffles I've ever tasted." She went quiet. "I hope she's okay."

"I'm certain she is."

"Then why haven't they found her, or Hayley? What if she's been trying to contact me on my phone? Oh god, I never thought about that! You took the battery to boost the signal for your communicator, but you never put it back."

"The alterations I made to your phone made it inoperable. I'm sorry. But when they are found, or reach out to the Pyrosian office on Earth, we'll be told. You are listed as being on board the Firebrand, alive and well, and so is Melody."

"Which means they haven't been found yet, nor have they tried to find me." She popped an entire candy into her mouth, making her next words come out muffled. "I hate this. I feel completely helpless. Worse, I feel guilty because I keep forgetting about everything and everyone but you. This Scorching thing is making me crazy."

He wrapped his arm around her shoulders and drew her in against his chest. "I know, but there is nothing either of us can do. The mating fever always makes it difficult to think, and we resisted it too long. That always makes the first cycle more intense. For now, we will have to pray to the Gods to watch over them."

"Do your gods ever answer prayers?"

He smiled down at her. "Of course. How else do you think I found you?"

"Your king sent his son here to steal a queen and you went along for the ride."

"But that's not the whole story. He sent scouts out into deep space, and one of them discovered a species who already carried our races' DNA. I don't believe that happened by accident. Humans have reached a dangerous point in their evolution. One that not all species survive. With our guidance, your race will continue to evolve and prosper."

"And in return, you'll have access to the women you need to avoid extinction."

He nodded. "Is that such a bad thing?"

Aria cocked her head to one side, the motion allowing some of her hair to spill across his chest. "I suppose not. Though I still think you need to be more open about everything."

"You can take that up with the princess. Remember, I do not make the laws. I simply protect the son of the man who does."

"Which means he trusts you. I think you might have more influence than you realize, you're just too honourable to think of using that to your advantage." She offered him one of the chocolates. "This one has caramel and sea salt. I think you'll like it."

He bowed his head, taking the candy from her hand with a slow swipe of his tongue. "Delicious."

"You haven't even bitten into it yet."

"I know," he said, trying to enunciate with his teeth stuck into the square. "I wasn't talking about the chocolate." The taste of his mate blended with the confection that was slowly melting on his tongue, creating a flavour that would forever remind him of this moment. He took a handful of the chocolates and gleefully rubbed them over her breasts, watching with pleasure as they melted on her skin.

"What are you doing, besides making a mess?" she asked, swatting playfully at his hands.

"Making dessert." He stroked a sticky finger over her lips, leaving a smear of chocolate behind. "I'm going to start right here, then work my way down until you are clean again."

Desire burned in her dazzling eyes as she reached for another chocolate, biting off one corner to expose a creamy pink substance inside. "In that case, I think you'd taste very nice mixed with cherry truffle." She marked his chest with the candy, and within seconds they were tangled together and laughing, both of them covered in chocolate as they rapidly emptied the box. It was the messiest, most glorious moment of his life.

———————

CHAPTER SEVEN

———————

ARIA WAS LOUNGING in the luxuriously big tub she'd discovered in the bathroom of their quarters. She and Tarjen had made use of it several times in the last few days, but this time she bathed alone. After almost two days of togetherness, she was enjoying a few moments to herself. The Scorching had faded enough she could think clearly again, so she was contemplating her future and praying for news about Piper. The entire arena had been thoroughly searched, and there was no sign of her anywhere. At least Haley was safe. She'd gotten word yesterday that her friend had been brought on board one of the ships for medical treatment and was doing fine. She'd asked Tarjen to relay messages to her, but so far there had been no reply.

Tarjen believed her sister was also among the wounded being cared for on the other Pyrosian ships, but as time passed, Aria's doubts grew. She didn't share Tarjen's faith that his Gods would make things right.

The only good news she'd had the last while was about Eva, the sweet woman that Keth had found injured and trapped in the rubble. She was going to be okay. Tarjen had said that was the will of the Gods, too.

His steadfast beliefs were one of the things she liked about him, along with his kindness and devotion. And she did like him, a lot. He was everything she'd hoped to find, and it scared the hell out of her. Was he really all he seemed to be, or would he change once she and Melody were on Pyros? God, was she really thinking about moving to another planet to be with someone she barely knew? Dating on Earth was hard, but surely there was a nice, human guy out there for her somewhere.

She slumped against the back wall of the tub and looked around her. Everything was familiar but different. The towels were made of a fabric she didn't recognize. The faucets and plumbing were shaped differently, and it had taken her a moment to figure out how things worked. Everything around her acted as a reminder that this was not her world, even though the man who claimed to be her life mate believed it would be. Was love a strong enough reason to leave everything--her friends, her practice--and follow Tarjen across the galaxy? Did Pyrosians even believe in love? Now that the mating madness was fading, would they be bound together forever with nothing in common but the memory of a few amazing days of sex? "I'm not leaving without Piper," she said quietly, making it a statement in a sea of questions.

Feeling more confused and conflicted than ever, she rose from the water and stepped out of the tub. Once the ship sensed her departure, it drained the water and dispatched several cleaning droids to clean the tub. "Now, that part of living on another planet would certainly be tempting. I'd never have to scrub another toilet."

She was still towelling off when she heard a familiar giggle coming from the main room. She moved closer to the door, listening to her daughter coo and babble at the man who wanted to be her father. The fact he'd gone to the nursery on his own and brought Melody back banished some of her doubts.

Alien or not, he was a good man.

"When your mother gets out of the bath, I think you're going in next, little star. You are wearing more of your meal than you consumed," Tarjen's voice was rife with amusement.

She was about to open the door and announce she was already out of the bath when he started speaking again. "You will have to learn better table manners if you are to dine with the royal family in future. They have high expectations, you know. Maggie and Gwen have already suggested that you be tutored with their children, at the palace. That is a great honour. We will have to see to it you are registered as a citizen as soon as we arrive home. They'll take a tiny bit of your blood, and one day, when you're old enough, they will tell you who you are matched to, and then you will be happy and mated like your mother and me. We will raise you to be a female any male would be proud to have as a mate. You are going to have a good life. I will see to it."

She flailed wildly at the door panel, trying to get it to open. When the door finally opened, she flew through it, wet, mostly naked, and angry. Tarjen was sitting on the bed, dressed in his uniform, with Melody lying beside him in a red and gold outfit that Aria had never seen before. "What do you mean, my daughter will be raised to be a female a man would be proud to mate with? She's not a broodmare, she's a human being! And what's this about her being registered? I never agreed to that. When she's old enough, she can decide for herself who she's going to love, and what her life will be like. We both have free will, Tarjen. Just because you and your Gods think I'm supposed to be with you, doesn't mean it's going to happen just like that!" she snapped her fingers for emphasis.

He gaped at her in confusion. "All Pyrosians are registered citizens. It is the law."

"I am not Pyrosian, and neither is Melody." She grabbed for clothes as she talked, pulling on a pair of loose fitting pants and a flowing red top from the assortment Tarjen had provided her.

"But you will be. We are mated, after all. This is all part of my plan."

"A blue spark and great sex aren't the same as agreeing to abandon my life here and follow you across the galaxy. I still get a choice, and I will fight to my last breath to make sure my daughter does, too." She felt a strange surge of emotions that ran counter to what she was feeling. Confusion. Hurt. Dismay. It didn't make sense, because all she was sure she was feeling right now was anger.

"The Gods choose our mates, not us."

"No!" She gathered Melody into her arms, cradling her close. "*Your* gods may choose for you, but I need a little more to go on than that. If I came with you, where would we live? Could I ever come back to Earth? Would Melody be allowed to leave Pyros? I have so many questions."

"Then ask them, and I will do my best to answer. You must understand, though, that we are bound together forever. There is no going back from this." He reached for her, but she pulled back, out of his reach.

"But I didn't get a choice! I didn't even want to meet you, remember? It was an accident. How can one mistake lead to this? And don't you dare say that it's the will of the gods."

He scowled his expression so easily read she could actually feel his frustration. "But it is!"

"If that's the only answer you can give me, then there's no need for us to talk anymore. I need to be alone."

"Don't go. Please, *seska*. Stay with me."

The sense of hurt and confusion hit her again, and she finally realized that he was the source of the emotions she sensed. Overwhelmed, she took another step back. "Why am I feeling what you're feeling? What new weirdness is this?"

"It is the bond I spoke of. It is different with each

couple. Some can read each other's thoughts from great distances, while some never sense more than the other's presence. It will take time to learn how strong our bond will be." He touched his chest, over his heart, then his head. "You will be with me here, and here. And I will always be with you."

She had reached her breaking point. "You mean we're going to be psychically linked, forever? And you didn't think to mention that ahead of time?"

He started to speak and she cut him off with a sharp shake of her head while Melody wailed, distressed by the loud voices and her mother's anger. "No. Just. No. I can't do this right now."

She walked out, somehow managing to get the door to activate on her first try. He didn't follow her, which should have made her happy, but part of her wasn't. *I'm a total freaking mess.*

She was three steps away from the door when it occurred to her she had no idea where to go. The only place she'd visited since arriving was the nursery. Where could she take a crying baby on a spaceship? Did they have lounges? Maybe a cafeteria? She took another step, uncertain, and registered a new sensation. Cold feet. Great. She'd been so mad she left without putting on her shoes.

She was still linked with Tarjen, and his emotional state wasn't much better than hers. If she went back for her shoes, she'd have to deal with him, and she didn't have that in her, not right now.

A door opened to her left, and Gwen stuck her head

out into the corridor. "You were right, Lisa, she's here," Gwen called back into the room before offering Aria an understanding smile. "I see you've hit the post-Scorching crisis phase. Feel like talking about it?"

"There are phases? Why didn't anyone tell me that? I swear, there needs to be a handbook. 'What to expect when your mate is an alien.' I bet it would be a bestseller."

"Maybe you can write it." Gwen gestured her closer. "Come on in. I'll tell Lisa to break into her stash of herbal teas. Peppermint or chamomile?"

"Peppermint, please." Her plan to be alone evaporated as she followed Gwen into the nursery. She needed answers. Maybe Gwen and the others could provide them. They had all chosen to stay with their mates. There had to be a reason they'd made that choice.

SHE WAS GONE. Tarjen paced the length of their quarters as he tried to work out where it had gone wrong. He'd made so many plans, arranged everything so that Aria would feel welcome and happy. Earth was a chaotic, dangerous place. He'd thought she'd welcome the security he offered. Instead, she'd reacted as if he were taking her freedom away. She didn't trust him, nor did she accept that this was the will of the Gods. Where had he gone wrong? He'd spent days working out his plans, trying to anticipate every possible problem. How had it all fallen apart? More importantly, what should he do now?

Frustrated, he continued pacing. Where was she? Where could she go? She didn't know the ship. Was she lost? Would she try and leave? No one would let that happen, but it bothered him to think she might attempt it. Finally, he forced himself to stop moving. If she could sense his emotions, then perhaps he could sense hers, too.

He felt a pull and turned toward it. She was located in that direction. He could feel it. Pleased, he tried again, and caught a whisper of emotion that wasn't his. Anger, doubt, fear, and guilt. She felt all the same things he did, but there were differences. It was gone a heartbeat later, overwhelmed by his desire to fix what he had done and make her happy again.

An alert chimed, announcing that he had a visitor. He wanted it to be Aria, but he sensed it wasn't. Puzzled, he opened the door. Joran stood outside, along with Vadir and Kash. All of them were grinning.

"So, things didn't go according to plan for you either, huh?" Vadir asked in Pyrosian.

"How do you know that?" Tarjen replied in the same language. After several days of speaking English, it felt odd to be speaking his own tongue again.

"Our mates sent us over here to help you. Apparently, they are with Aria right now, and no, you're not allowed to go over there. They were very clear about that." Joran entered the room and the others trailed in after him.

"Actually, they made it clear none of us were welcome," Kash grumbled.

"But, Joran is the crown prince. He can go where he pleases. It's his ship."

Vadir chuckled. "And I'm rich enough to buy and sell planets if I wanted. It doesn't make any difference to our mates, though. There are times when their word is law."

Tarjen folded his arms over his chest. "The law is the law."

"And that right there is why you're alone in your quarters and your mate is down the hall not talking to you. To quote my *tani*, I've been there, done that, and got the T-shirt." Vadir sat down in one of the chairs, looking annoyingly smug.

"I have no idea why you would want clothing made to commemorate a problem like this, but if you have advice for me, it would seem I could use some. I had a plan, but it isn't working." He raised his hands in a gesture of confusion. "Why didn't it work?"

Joran claimed the other chair, while Kash leaned against the wall near the door as if he didn't trust that Tarjen would stay in the room. Tarjen sat down on the corner of the bed and looked at the others expectantly.

"It didn't work because you made the same mistake we did." Joran said. "When I found Maggie, I made the mistake of forgetting that while I had been raised with an understanding of the Scorching and the instant connection between mates, she had no idea what any of it meant. She felt like she had no choice."

"Aria mentioned, choice, too. I tried to explain it was the will of the Gods, but it didn't help."

"It wouldn't," Vadir stated as if it should have been obvious. "I've spent more time dealing with humans than anyone else from our planet, and I can tell you that most of them place a high value on having the freedom to choose. If you corner or coerce them, they react badly. Plus, their beliefs are many and varied. They don't all believe in the same gods, and many don't believe in gods at all." Vadir shrugged. "They're complicated."

Joran leaned back in his chair. "Maggie mentioned that your mate had concerns about her daughter being raised on Pyros. What's that about?"

"She does not want Melody registered as a citizen. She is concerned that not only am I taking away her choices, but I will take away Melody's, too. I tried to explain, but she took the child and left. I didn't know about Melody. I didn't plan for her, but now I know, I want what's best for her. Above all else, I want her to be happy."

The prince closed his eyes and groaned. "We didn't consider what would happen if one of the matches already had children. Since our females cannot conceive with anyone but their true mate, it never occurred to us. My father will have to make some decisions about that, and I imagine he'll want to speak to your mate and the other females before he does so."

"If she comes to Pyros at all. She is very unhappy right now." Tarjen touched his temple. "I can sense her emotions, and she can sense mine. Another detail I forgot to mention to her ahead of time."

Kash winced. "Things would go better if the humans had more information about our world and how matings work between our species."

"Aria said the same thing," Tarjen agreed. "She has many questions. I hope your mates will be able to give her answers. If she chooses to stay…" he trailed off.

"Then you would be put in the same position she is now in. It's something we don't have to deal with on Pyros anymore, because mates know months or even years in advance who they will bond with, and they make arrangements before they ever meet. We need to find a better way to arrange things," Joran said.

"Yes. And whatever our plans are, it won't include coming back to Earth. Not after what happened this time." Kash slapped his hand against his thigh in irritation. "Considering the damage, it is amazing that only a few males died. The humans are scrambling to explain how it happened and apologize, but we can't risk another attack. The bombers who survived have all been captured, but so far none of the leaders have been located. The ones who planted the devices thought they were working alone. They believed they were only going to cause minor damage. Their goal was to spread fear, not commit murder."

"Which means the real danger lies with the leaders," Tarjen said.

Joran nodded. "Once we find Vadir's missing guest,

the only trips anyone will be making to Earth is to escort the females as they pack for their new home."

"What missing guest?" Tarjen asked. It bothered him to be so out of touch. His job normally required regular briefings. He should have been briefed about the group threatening the Gathering, too. How could he protect his mate and their daughter if he didn't have all the facts?

"The Romaki Prince, Radek. He hasn't been seen since the bombings," Kash said.

"Him? I saw him transform and take flight during the attack. How is it no one has seen him? In his dragon form, he's difficult to miss." A thought crossed Tarjen's mind. "Is there any chance he might have taken the missing human female with him?"

Vadir groaned. "If he did, I'll skin him and nail his hide to the wall of my office."

"Is that likely?" Kash asked.

Vadir answered. "Humans have legends about dragons. It's one of the reasons Radek is here. You know his people never leave their homeworld anymore. It's been centuries since they abandoned space travel. They're convinced that if they leave Romak, they'll lose their magic and never find their way home again, just like the colony ships they lost."

"Well, clearly Radek hasn't lost his magic, or he wouldn't have been able to transform." Kash pointed out.

"Which means he's got some pretty big news to share when I return him home. If we ever find him."

Vadir pinched his chin. "You know, if he's got one of the missing females with him, that would explain why he hasn't been in contact. Romaki matings are even more intense than Pyrosian."

Joran muttered under his breath. "Wonderful. The humans will be so pleased to know there's another species out there interested in claiming their females. You're right, Kash. We're not going to be coming back to Earth any time soon."

Something clicked into place in Tarjen's mind. "Whether you return or not, you will need someone on Earth to coordinate future matings and stay in contact with the humans. If Aria will not come to Pyros, I will volunteer to stay behind. I do not wish to be separated from her. I cannot protect her if I am on the other side of the galaxy."

All three men looked at him, but only Joran spoke. "You'd be a target if you stayed."

"So will she. If she stays, so will I."

Vadir pointed to the door. "Then go tell her that."

He rose to his feet, tugged his uniform into place and said a silent prayer to the Gods that this went better than the last conversation he had with Aria. He had to make her understand that he would do whatever it took to be with her, even if it meant leaving his family, friends, and career behind. After all, he'd expected her to do the same for him.

CHAPTER EIGHT

Talking with the other women had been enlightening for Aria. They shared the challenges they'd overcome after the Scorching had ended and they each had to face the reality that their lives were irrevocably changed. It made her feel better about her own situation. Their mates had made mistakes, too, but they had found a way to work through it, and none of them regretted leaving Earth.

"And they love you? It's not just lust?" she asked them.

"I know Joran loves me, and it's clear to anyone with eyes that Kash worships the ground Gwen walks on," Maggie said.

"Vee loves me. He's still learning how to show it, but I know he does." Lisa sat across from her, a cup of tea in one hand and a partially eaten cupcake in the other.

"It's your decision, but if you come back with us,

you could be a huge help." Maggie gestured to herself. "Before all this, I was a barista, Gwen sold books, and Lisa drew caricatures and local landscape paintings for tourists. We've done our best, but none of us have your qualifications. I know you were kidding about needing a how-to manual, but we're going to need *something* to give to new arrivals. Cognitive augmentation will give them the language and a basic understanding of how things work, but the culture shock is still pretty harsh."

It was an interesting idea, but before she agreed to anything, she needed to talk to Tarjen and figure out if they could make things work. "Maybe."

"I know. You still need to talk to your mate. I can promise you this much, though. Melody will always have the right to choose. I will personally guarantee it. Whatever decree King Janus eventually makes regarding children born on Earth, Melody will always be free to return to Earth, to chose her own mate, or to live as a Pyrosian."

Some of the tension locked around her ribs eased, making it easier for Aria to breathe. "Thank you."

Maggie touched her rounded stomach. "Your little girl has given all of us something to think about. I hope for the sake of Pyros that Hope, Melody, and my future daughter choose to stay and help rebuild the population, but that choice should be theirs to make, not ours."

Lisa raised her cup in a toast. "To the next generation. Your little girls…and my son."

Everyone gasped and then the room erupted into

questions. "What? When? How far along? A boy? You're having a boy?"

Aria sat back in her chair, overwhelmed by emotions that weren't her own. *What the hell is happening now?*

Lisa was chattering away happily, and for the moment none of them had noticed Aria's distress. "We were going to tell everyone on the way home. I only found out a few days ago. Torel confirmed it for me. We're having a little boy. Vee is over the moons and can't wait to get home so he can start building a new wing for the kid. He's already working on the plans, and we're going to make some changes to his ship so junior can come with us when we travel for work."

"That's wonderful news! I'm so happy! Our babies are going to grow up together and be the best of friends, just like we are," Gwen declared.

Another wave of emotions slammed into Aria, and she closed her eyes, trying to find some kind of equilibrium.

"Aria? You okay?" Gwen asked.

"I'm not sure. I was sitting here and suddenly I could feel all your emotions. All of you. It was a little overwhelming."

Lisa uttered a yelp of delight. "We've got another psychic! Yes! Have you always been an empath, or is this a new development?"

Opening her eyes, Aria found herself the focus of everyone's attention. "It's new. Sorry, Lisa. I didn't mean to distract from your good news. I started sensing

Tarjen's feelings this morning, and now this. I'm not sure how many more surprises I can take."

"I get it." Lisa came over to pat her shoulder. "I was always clairvoyant, but I couldn't read thoughts until after Vee and I were mated. It took some getting used to."

"We really do need a manual," Gwen muttered.

"How is it now? Are you still sensing all of us?" Lisa asked.

Aria focused for a moment, but all she was getting was a general sense of happiness from the three of them, along with an undertone of concern. "It's better now. I think it was just the sudden spike of elation when you shared your good news, Lisa. Congratulations, by the way."

Maggie was still looking at her intently. "You're a psychologist, right? And now, you're a psychologist with empathic abilities."

Gwen hummed in approval. "Are you thinking what I'm thinking?"

Maggie nodded. "I'm starting to think that these Pyrosian Gods know what they're doing. Don't tell Joran I said that, though. He'd start saying I told you so." The princess turned her attention back to Aria. "If you decide to come to Pyros, I think you'd be a huge asset. We need someone to help with the new arrivals as they adjust to their new lives. I'm not sure how it would work just yet, but would you think about it?"

Helping people to cope with loss and change was why she'd become a grief counsellor in the first place.

"I'll think about it, but I'm not making any promises. It's not just Tarjen I'm worried about. I don't want to leave my little sister behind. I'm all she's got."

"If she wants to come to Pyros, she can. I wouldn't have left Earth without Gwen and Lisa, and they wouldn't have left without me." Maggie spoke with utter confidence, and Aria believed her. It was nice to know that she had a princess on her side.

"Thank you," she said. After that, they went back to chatting about babies, pregnancy, and the futures their children might have. Aria listened more than she talked, still working through everything she'd learned. It was a lot to take in.

After a while, something new started pressing in on her awareness. It only took her a moment to recognize the feeling. *Tarjen.* She could sense him. It wasn't like before, when his emotions were pouring into her. This was focused. Like a voice gently calling her name. Without really being aware of it, she set down her tea and stood. "Congratulations, Lisa. And thank you all so much. I need to go, now. Tarjen wants to talk to me."

"Your bond is strengthening," Gwen noted with a nod of approval. "We'll keep Melody here and give her a bath while you're gone. Lisa and Maggie could both use the practice."

"Kick butt and take no prisoners. You got this," Lisa said, holding her cupcake aloft like a sword.

"Tarjen is one of the best men I've ever known, on any planet. I hope you two find a way to work through this. He needs someone to remind him there's more to life than duty and planning." Maggie rose and gave her a quick hug. "And you deserve someone who will treat you and Melody like princesses."

There was a lump in her throat as she said goodbye and left the nursery. If going to Pyros meant having friends like those three around, maybe it would be worth the risk.

She stepped into the hall and was nearly knocked over by a woman running headlong down the corridor.

"Sorry! I'm trying to find the nursery. Where is it? Oh my god. Aria? Is that you?"

"Haley?" Aria got her bearings and looked up. Her missing friend was standing in front of her, her normally perfect auburn curls were mussed, and her eyes were…shit. "You're mated to a Pyrosian?" She blurted out her question as she stared at her friend's glowing eyes. They weren't brown anymore. They were a stunning shade of gold.

"And so are you! I'm glad you said yes." She glanced up, eyes widening as she looked over Aria's shoulder. "Whoa, is that him? He's way cuter in person."

She didn't need to look to know it was Tarjen. Her focus was on her friend. "How did you get here? How are you mated?"

"Aria? Is this your missing friend?" Tarjen asked as he came up behind them.

"Hi, I'm Haley. You must be Tarjen. Torel just told me you were on board this ship, Aria. I knew you were safe, but no one told me you were so close. Or maybe they did and I forgot. the Scorching…"

"I know. I had a hard time thinking straight, too. Even when I was worried about you and Piper. When Tarjen told me you'd been found and were safe, I was so relieved. I just wish you'd found a way to tell me sooner."

Haley blushed and hung her head. "Sorry. There was a lot going on. I'll explain soon, I promise. I'm not supposed to be out of bed right now, but when I found out you and Melody were here, I had to come find you."

"Wait, why aren't you supposed to be out of bed? What happened? Do you know where Piper is?"

"I got hit with some shrapnel from the bombings. I don't remember it, but apparently, I had a skull fracture and some internal bleeding. I'm fine, now, though. Really. Pyrosian medicine is seriously impressive. As for Piper, I don't know what happened to her. Once the first bomb went off, we ran for it. She was behind me when we both got caught in a blast. Part of the stadium smacked me in the head, and that's all I remember. I'm sorry. I don't know where she is. No one seems to." Haley's face fell. "I should have made her go ahead. I wasn't able to run very fast in my heels, but she wouldn't leave me."

"It's not your fault." Aria said, her voice breaking slightly.

Tarjen's hand touched her shoulder. "I think I know where Piper is. If I am correct, then she is safe."

"Where is she? Why hasn't she contacted anyone?"

"She's with Radek. At least, I think that's where she is. No one has seen him since the bombing either."

"Then how do you know that she's fine? They could both be hurt!"

He shook his head. "There is nothing on this planet that could injure the prince. He's not Pyrosian. He's something far more powerful."

"My sister is with another alien? Is he dangerous?" She didn't know whether to be relieved or panicked at the news.

"He's probably one of the most dangerous creatures in existence, but he won't harm your sister. If she's with him, then she is likely his mate, and there is nothing in the universe a Romaki ice dragon wouldn't do to protect what's theirs."

Her stomach twisted into a fresh set of knots. "A dragon?! Why is Piper with a fucking dragon? They're mythical!"

Haley started to giggle, then guffaw.

"This isn't funny," Aria snapped.

Haley managed to stop laughing long enough to reply. "Oh honey, it is. You just can't see it yet. Of all the men in the galaxy, only your sister could snag herself a damned *dragon*."

She had a point. "Why haven't they been in contact?"

"When Radek transformed, he probably lost his communicator."

"Transformed? He's a shapeshifting dragon? You

need to explain this to me, because I'm having trouble wrapping my head around the idea my sister's dating a scaly dude who breathes fire and can fly."

"In bipedal form, Romaki dragons do not have scales, and I believe that Radek is a member of the ice dragon clan, which means his breath weapon is ice, not fire. Otherwise, your assessment is accurate enough."

Another Pyrosian appeared in the corridor, his golden eyes locked on Haley. "Why is it you insist on defying my every instruction, *otama*? You are supposed to be in our quarters, resting before the Scorching takes hold again."

"And I'll be there soon, but I had to find Aria." Haley beamed at the new arrival, looking happier than Aria had ever seen her. "Torel, this is Aria. Aria, this is Torel, my…mate."

Tarjen bumped a fist to the blonde Pyrosian's shoulder. "Congratulations. Gold suits you."

Torel grinned. "Same to you." Then he turned to Haley and scooped her into his arms. "Say goodbye to your friend now. You are going back to bed, and this time I will personally see to it that you don't leave it again until I give you permission."

Haley yelped. "You are not the boss of me. Mate, not master, remember?"

Torel's response was a low wordless growl.

Haley waved at her. "I think we're going, now. We'll talk soon, and don't worry about Pi. That girl can take care of herself. I'll see you after this Scorching thing finally wears off. Bye!"

Tarjen watched them go, his mouth open and eyes wide.

"That was quite the exit, wasn't it?" she asked.

"I have never known Torel to act that way. Mating has made him more…"

"Aggressive? Possessive? Over the top Alpha? I've never seen Haley like that, either." She could feel her friend's emotions, too. They were too powerful to ignore. Haley had finally allowed herself to be happy.

"Then their mating will be an interesting one." Tarjen looked down at her, his expression softer now. "Will you return to our quarters with me? There are matters I'd like to discuss with you in private."

"I know. I heard you call to me. That's why I was out here." She took his hand. "Let's talk."

THE MOMENT they were through the door to their quarters, Tarjen turned to face Aria and dropped to his knees. "I want to apologize. For me, being mated is the cumulation of a lifetime of hopes and planning. I forgot to consider that for you, it would be something new and strange. I swear on my honour that I will not make that mistake again."

"And I'm sorry I walked away from you. You were willing to talk, and I wasn't. If this is going to work, we're going to need to talk, a lot."

He could sense the truth of her words, as well as the hope and fear churning inside her. "Do you want this to work, *seska*? If you do, then I will do whatever it takes to make you happy. If that means staying on Earth with you, then I will do that. I've already told my prince."

Her emotions spiked into shock and delight. "You'd stay on my uncivilized world for me?"

He took both her hands in his. "I will do whatever it takes to make you happy. I want our mating to be blessed with laughter and joy. That can happen anywhere, but only if we're together. None of this is how I planned it, but I'm starting to understand that there are some things in life that cannot be planned. They simply happen, and I need to accept that. Would you stay with me and help me learn how?"

Her eyes shimmered with tears, and he thought he might have screwed things up again, but then she smiled. "I don't know where I want to live, yet. That's a big decision we should make together. But, I do know that I want to live with you."

"In that case, there's something I meant to ask you. I planned on doing this much sooner, but since I met you, my plans have a tendency to blow up."

She laughed. "You did the same to me. I wasn't even going to accept this match, and now here I am, mated to an alien."

He released one of her hands and reached into his pocket. He'd only remembered about the ring this morning, and since then, there had been no opportunity to do what he should have on that first day. He took out the ring and placed it on the palm of his hand before offering it to her. "I know we are already mated, but I bought this ring because I wanted you to know that your customs are as important as mine. I forgot that, and I am sorry. Will you wear my ring and agree to be my wife, as well as my mate?"

She didn't say anything for so long he wondered if he'd done the ritual wrong, even though the only emotions he got from her were joy and excitement. Finally, she took the ring from his hand and nodded. "Yes. I'll marry you."

She slipped the ring onto her left hand, then held it up to see it better. "It's beautiful. I've never seen a stone like that."

"It's from Pyros. My father is an engineer at one of the sites where it's mined."

"You had this made before even left?"

"I did. I had it all planned…" he shrugged and rose to his feet. "Then the bombs went off."

"And everything changed." She stepped in close and placed her hands on his chest. "It's customary for the couple to kiss after she has accepted his proposal."

"I like this custom." He pulled her in close and kissed her, savouring the moment. Her lips were sweet and slightly sticky, as if she'd been eating chocolate again. She stood on her toes and kissed him back, opening her mouth to his with a moan that made his balls tighten and his heart sing.

Their tongues danced and their bodies moved together, creating a fire that not even an ocean could douse. His started tugging at her clothes, needing to be skin to skin. She started trying to undress him, too, but her fingers stumbled over the unfamiliar clasps.

"Your uniform is fighting me," she muttered between kisses.

"You get naked, I'll get this off," he replied, then kissed her one last time before stepping away. He undid the closures without looking, not wanting to take his eyes off of Aria. She blushed as she stripped, but this time she didn't try to hide from him.

He kicked off his shoes, his pants, and then he prowled the short distance back to her side and lifted her into his arms. She pressed an open-mouthed kiss to his chest as he carried her to the bed, set her down, and then stretched out beside her.

He drew her back into his arms for a slow, torrid kiss that didn't end until both of them were breathing hard. Aria reached for him, sliding her hands through his hair as she threw her leg over his and drew them together until his cock was pressed against her mons.

"Is this the Scorching again? I feel like I'm on fire."

"No, *seska*. The Scorching has passed. This is how it will always be between us."

She lifted her head to grin at him. "Then I'm even happier that I said yes."

"As am I." He rolled her onto her back and moved to cover her, the need to be inside her almost as intense as it had been the first time.

She nuzzled his neck, nibbling and sucking her way up to his ear. When she reached his lobe, she gave it a delicate nip. "Flames, that feels good."

She nipped him again, and he bucked his hips against her, letting the tip of his cock slide along her pussy. He turned his head and captured her mouth with his, letting his tongue slide between her lips to tangle with hers. His hands found her breasts, and he started to toy with them, loving the way she gasped and arched beneath him with every gentle tweak.

"More, she gasped, and he happily complied, kissing his way down her body until he could suck and lap at her nipples. One hand drifted lower, following the soft lines of her body down to where his cock met her pussy. He slid a finger inside her until he found her clit and started rubbing it in slow circles.

She quivered and squirmed beneath this double assault, and every moan and gasp had him aching to bury himself inside her. He held himself back, though. Before he claimed her, he wanted to watch her reach her climax. It didn't take long. Soon she was on the brink, and all it took to push her over the edge was a gentle pinch of her clit. She came with a wild cry of his name.

She was still panting when she opened her eyes and tugged lightly on his hair. "I want you, Tarjen. Please?"

"Whatever it takes to make my mate happy." He shifted his weight over her, using his arms to keep most of his weight off of her as she raised her knees and opened herself to him.

He buried himself to the hilt in one slow, steady thrust, a groan of pure pleasure tearing from his throat. "Mine."

She nodded, and he felt the full force of her

emotions hit him for the first time. She gasped, and he knew that she was sensing him, too. Somewhere in the maelstrom, they found each other and held on, a blending of souls as well as bodies.

He lost all control, pounding into her with urgent thrusts as the combined weight of their emotions overcame him. Lust. Need. Joy. Acceptance. They were all fuel to his desires. He drove into her, hips pumping in a wild tempo that didn't stop until he reached climax and exploded, his cock swelling and locking into place as he came.

He stared down at Aria, her face flushed and her hair spread out across his pillows, and thanked the Gods for bringing her and Melody into his life.

"I'm happy they brought us to you, too." She whispered.

"You heard that?"

"Of course I did, you said it very clearly."

"No, my little beauty. I didn't say anything at all. Our bond has grown even stronger. We are truly one, now."

"That's going to take some getting used to."

"Yes, it is. But I think it will help us communicate much better, don't you?"

She laughed. "It most certainly will."

The Gods had given them everything they needed to face their new life together. Nothing had gone according to plan, but as his beloved mate had pointed out, they'd found their way to happiness in the end.

EPILOGUE

"AND YOU'RE sure the message said they'd be arriving soon?" Aria asked for the hundredth time. She knew she was fretting, but she couldn't help it. She wouldn't calm down until she'd seen for herself that Piper was fine.

"I'm sure, *seska*."

"Then where are they? Surely we'd be able to see them by now." She pointed out the massive doors of the docking bay to the emptiness beyond. It was strange to be looking down at Earth, but she could see it clearly through the forcefield that covered the open doors.

Tarjen cradled Melody in his arms, rocking her gently as Aria paced the deck in front of him. "They'll be here."

It was the day after Tarjen's proposal, and she'd spent a long night worrying about Piper before they finally received word that she and the missing prince had been located.

Haley was still locked away with Torel. Apparently, they hadn't met until some time after she and Tarjen had, and they were both still under the thrall of the Scorching. She wouldn't be able to talk to her friend properly until this evening at the earliest.

While they'd been waiting for word on her sister, she and Tarjen had talked. It was far easier to come to an understanding when they could sense each other's emotions.

In the end, she had agreed to move to Pyros. It was the only safe choice. On Earth, Tarjen would be in constant danger, and her eyes would make her a target for anyone in the anti-alien faction. That meant Melody would be at risk, too. It didn't make sense to stay.

They'd talked about other things, too. They'd be living at the palace, which meant Melody would be able to grow up with Hope, just as Lisa had predicted. Tarjen had encouraged her to work with Gwen and the others to create a better system for helping the human females adjust. Her life on Pyros was starting to take shape.

"We are coming back to Earth though, right?" she asked, glancing at Maggie.

"*Seska...* we talked about this. It's not safe," Tarjen replied.

"Then we need to find a way to make it safe," Maggie declared. "Joran, you promised me I'd be able to return to Earth. We don't need to do another Gathering. In fact, it might be better if we took in smaller batches of human women more often, without any fanfare."

Kash opened his mouth to speak, but stopped when Gwen glared at him. "Don't even think about it, my love. Our daughter will want to see Earth one day, and so will the rest of the children born to human mothers. I know there are risks, but you can't tell us we're never going to see Earth again."

"You made this decision without talking to any of us,"Maggie pointed out. "Did you really think we'd just agree with you and never go back again?"

"We didn't decide anything. I'm not the king," Joran said.

"No, but you're related to the man who can." Maggie retorted.

"I don't want the ones who attacked us to think we're running scared. If they think they're winning, things will get worse. We've got plenty of time to come up with a plan while we're travelling back to Pyros, right?" Aria said.

Maggie and Gwen nodded in agreement, and the men all sighed.

Aria turned to look at Tarjen. "Don't look at me like that. You're the one who likes plans."

He smiled a little. "That I do."

"Look, there's the shuttle," Lisa said, pointing to the rapidly approaching ship. It was bright white, which made it easy to spot against the star-strewn sky.

"What's that?" Aria pointed to the darker shape that suddenly appeared in front of the shuttle's nose. The only reason she could see it was because it contrasted with the white hull.

"That…" Tarjen stared for a second. "I think that's the prince."

Another shape appeared beside the first one, this one slightly smaller. "If that's the prince, then what is that?" Aria asked.

The shuttle and its two companions soared through the open doors of the docking bay, and Aria got her first look at a living legend. There were two dragons on the flight deck, both of them bigger than the shuttle they'd accompanied inside. Their scales were an iridescent shades of blue and silver, and one of them swung its head around to look straight at her with eyes that were very familiar. *Piper*.

"Tarjen, I think your future sister-in-law is a dragon. Any idea how that happened?"

He shook his head, as astounded as she was. "None. But it should be an interesting story."

She leaned into him and he wrapped an arm around her shoulders, holding her close. Since meeting Tarjen, her whole life had become an interesting story, and she couldn't wait to find out what the next chapter held for all of them.

THE END

Want to read more stories with book boyfriends
that are out of this world?

**Check out Susan Hayes' other Science Fiction
Romance Titles**

<u>The Drift</u>
Double Down
All In
Wild Card
Three of a Kind
No Limit
Blind Bet
Aces Over Queen

<u>Nova Force</u>
Operation Phoenix
Operation Cobalt

<u>3013: The Series</u>
3013: RENEGADE
3013: STOWAWAY
3013: TARGETED
3013: FATED
3013: SCARRED

TOREL

Star-crossed Alien Mail Order Brides #5

What do you do when your planet runs out of women? Send for takeout, of course.

Torel is the best medical officer in the Pyrosian fleet, but being the best comes with a cost. When the queen personally orders him to apply to Star-Crossed Dating, he's relieved when there's no match for him among the human females of Earth. He doesn't have time for those kinds of distractions.

Mated or not, he's on his way to Earth to help the newly mated females adjust to the life awaiting them on Pyros. All he has to do is keep them healthy and happy during the voyage home. It should be the easiest assignment of his career.

This book contains a widow determined to never fall in love again, and a doctor who is about to discover that when it comes to the heart, he's still got a lot to learn.

A SNEAK PEAK AT TOREL

Haley ducked around a corner and then peeked back the way they'd come. It wasn't an idea vantage point, but a sports arena wasn't exactly designed with covert observation in mind. "Do you think she'll be okay?"

Piper joined her, watching her older sister, Aria, from their hiding spot.

"Now that she's through the gate? Yeah, I think so. I really hope she doesn't turn her match down before she gives him a chance, though."

"Me too," Haley agreed. "She's one of the kindest women I've ever know. I'd like to see her happy, even if that means she ends up on another planet." Aria had been assigned as Haley's grief counsellor, and over time their relationship had changed to one of sisterhood and friendship. Haley's world had shattered when she lost Eric to cancer, and Aria had been the rock she'd clung to while she grieved.

Piper sighed and swept a stray lock of her bright

blue hair out of her face. "I'm afraid that's one of the reasons she wants to say no. She doesn't want to leave us."

"I know." Haley weighed her next words carefully. "Will you be okay if she did go?"

Piper shot her a look of pure frustration. "Of course I'll be okay. I love my sister, but she needs to cut the apron string and focus on her life instead of mine."

"She worries about you, Pi."

"I know. And I know it comes from a place of love and all that, but I'm an adult, now. Have been for years. When is she going to stop mothering me?"

Haley patted the younger woman's shoulder. "How does never sound? Because even if she winds up on the far side of the galaxy, you know she's going to find a way to keep tabs on us both. Caring about others is Aria's superpower."

Piper nodded and glanced around the corner again. "She's headed inside. Guess this means we should go find our seats, huh? I hope we got a good view. I know I didn't get matched, but that doesn't mean I can't enjoy the view."

"I'm planning on enjoying the view, too. I don't want a match, but I wouldn't mind taking home one of those alien hotties for a few days."

The two of them followed the almost entirely female crowd through the corridors, keeping an eye out for signs pointing to their seating area. "You ever think you'll want more than a few days of fun with a guy?" Piper asked out of the blue.

"Nope. I already found the perfect guy once, and then I lost him to cancer. I can't go through that again. I'm a solo act from now on." She'd had her share of hurt and heartache for this lifetime. The thought of dating again, of trying to replace Eric, made her want to curl into a ball and hide.

"So that's it? You're done?"

"I'm not done with men, no. I just don't want to keep them. I'm sticking with the catch and release approach from now on."

Piper didn't comment until they had descended a flight of stairs and found their row. "I'm not sure I want that. I used to, but lately…"

Haley did a careful sidestep along the narrow space between the seats and questioned her choice to wear her new Prada heels today. They were gorgeous, but not exactly practical. "You're almost out of your twenties, now. I was about your age when I started re-thinking my plan to stay single forever. Suddenly I was almost thirty and I wanted more. I found it, too. Eric was the best thing that ever happened to. One day, I hope you find someone that makes you happy."

"Yeah, me too. That's why I took a chance with the Star-Crossed dating thing. It didn't work out, though."

"There's an entire planet of Pyrosian men looking for mates. Don't give up, yet." She sat down and scanned the scene in front of her. The domed roof of BC Place stadium was open, allowing the summer sun to fill the space with light. In the middle of the dome was a large, white, and elegantly decorated tent. Sitting beneath it were a large group of women, all dressed up and clearly nervous. None of them could keep still for long, and even from their elevated seats she could hear their high-pitched voices as they chatted with each other.

"Good point." Piper sat down beside her and tossed her bag into the empty seat to her left. "Do you think they have firefighters on their planet? I should probably date one in case the next place I get a job catches fire, too."

Haley winked at Piper. "Best fire insurance a girl can have. Those guys really no how to handle their hoses."

"Oh my god, I cannot believe you said that out loud. And my sister is worried *I'm* going to be a bad influenced on Melody." Piper was still laughing as she leaned forward in her chair and looked down at the arena floor. "Do you see Aria?"

"Near the front of the tent, looking like she's going to bolt at any second."

"She's not the only one who looks like they're having second thoughts. Me, I'd be admiring the scenery already on display." Piper pointed to where several tall, broad-shouldered men were standing at the edge of the stage that had been set up at one end of the arena.

The girl isn't wrong about the view. Haley took a moment to appreciate it for herself. It was the first time she had seen a Pyrosian in person, and the pictures she had seen didn't do them justice. She pulled out her phone and captured a few pictures of the aliens, then continued taking pictures of the rest of the arena. Officially she was here as a friend, but that didn't mean she couldn't take pictures and observe as much as she could about the Pyrosians and this event as she could.

There was a story here, she just wasn't sure what form it would take, yet. Everything seemed to be on the up-and-up, but any journalist worth her words knew that looks could be deceiving. The best stories were always buried deeper. Aria was here because she'd made a simple mis-click and accepted a match with an alien. She hadn't intended to do it, but there had been no undo button. Were the Pyrosians playing fair, or were there other women here who had been tricked into coming to meet their matches?

No one knew much about how the first human women had met their mates, either. Oh, sure, Haley had seen the promotional materials and ads that were all over television and the internet. There probably wasn't a human on the planet who hadn't at this point, but ads and copy didn't tell the truth, they crafted a message. Her father was constantly demanding that she prove herself to him, what better way to do that than to get the scoop of a lifetime about the first alien life to visit Earth?

If she thought there was something nefarious going on, she would never have encouraged Aria to come here today. It wasn't that she thought the Pyrosians were plotting the demise of humanity or anything, but everyone had secrets…and if she kept her eyes open, maybe she could uncover one or two of them. She was a good reporter, even if it wasn't her dream job. All her dreams had died with Eric.

She ended her internal musings as several more men appeared to one side of the stage. One was pale blond, the other had dark hair, and they were both wearing what looked like designer suits from Earth. They were accompanied by several serious looking soldiers wearing standard uniforms, and it was obvious that they were there to protect the new arrivals. These must be VIP's, and apparently, they knew how to dress for success here on Earth. A blonde woman in a flowing sundress of orange and yellow joined them a minute later. She walked right through the guards and up to the dark haired Pyrosian, kissing his cheek with obvious affection. It was hard to be sure, given the distance, but Haley thought the woman was human. In fact, she looked kind of familiar.

"Is that one of the women from the ads?" Piper asked.

Of course. That's why she recognized her. "I think so, yeah. So that guy she just smooched must be her mate."

"Too bad he's taken, he's easy on the eyes. Then again, so is that platinum blonde hottie beside him."

Haley raised her phone and used the camera feature to zoom in on the group just as they turned to greet another group of VIP's, this one followed by a camera crew. "Looks like the mayor has arrived."

"Must be getting close to show time, then," Piper replied.

Haley took a few photos, then used her phone to

zoom in Aria. She seemed to be alright, though she was still nervous. She thought about sending her a text message to let her know she wasn't alone, but Ri had her hands full keeping Melody entertained and happy so she decided against it.

When she looked back at the stage, things had changed. The crowd of VIP's had grown, and they were starting to take their seats in a roped off area to the right of the main stage. There were more uniformed Pyrosians appearing, now, and plenty of organizers running around, checking in with each other and then dashing off again.

It wasn't long before everyone and everything seemed to be in place. The Pyrosian soldiers were lined up in formation on each side of the stage, the guests were all seated, and a low chorus of gasps filled the arena as a ship descended out of the sky and through the open roof of the stadium. At the same time, the matched Pyrosian males started filing onto the stadium floor. They were all wearing matching outfits, and there were feminine murmurs of approval from all over the arena as they marched toward their places. As entrances go, it was damned impressive - right up to the moment the explosions started.

Torel Zinn had worked hard to become the official medical officer for the Pyrosian royal family. One of the benefits of his position was being able to attend to members of that family while they were aboard the fleet's flagship, the *Firebrand*. That benefit had allowed him to be present when the first human females were brought on board, and he'd been able to watch his friend and commander fall under the thrall of the Scorching.

Now, they were in orbit around Earth for a second time. He should be preparing for the arrival of the newly claimed human females assigned to the ship, but instead, he was sitting behind his desk, across from one of the richest males in the galaxy.

"You should come down with us, Torel. I'm taking my mate back to the sea wall where she used to work. It's a pretty spot, nice views, lots of people, and fresh air. Then, Lisa wants to introduce me to something called poutine. Fried carbohydrates smothered in meaty gravy and cheese. We're having it for lunch before heading to the stadium. You're welcome to join the three of us. In fact, it might be handy to have a doctor on hand, just in case this food doesn't agree with Pyrosian biology. What do you say? Want to stress test your heart?" Vadir asked, his golden eyes gleaming with an alarming level of amusement.

Torel had long since learned that when Vadir was this happy, he was usually up to something. Often, it was something bordering on illegal. Vadir had enough money, charm, and power to talk himself out of any trouble, Torel didn't. "Thanks for the offer, but I've been invited to join the Prince and Princess on their shuttle.

I'll see you at the ceremony, and I'll make sure to bring something for an upset stomach, just in case."

"Got anything that might help a Romaki's digestion?" Vadir asked casually.

"Why would I need…." Torel stared at Vadir with dawning alarm. "By the Flames of the First Ones, what have you done this time? Romaki dragons haven't left their homeworld for hundreds of years. Why would I need to treat one?"

Vadir winked and leaned back in his chair. "One dragon did. He's been staying out of sight on my ship since we met up with the *Firebrand*. And before you ask, yes, Joran knows he's here. We've been keeping it quiet, obviously, but he's attending the ceremony as my guest."

Well, that explained why Vadir looked so happy. He was about to introduce humanity to yet another alien species that might have had previous contact with Earth sometime in their distance past. No doubt he'd be doing all he could to broker more trade deals between the three planets during this visit.

"Do his leaders know he's here? What if he's injured? No one knows much about treating a Romaki. There's no need, since they're bound by law not to leave the planet."

"He's a *dragon*. I'm not sure there's a weapon on Earth that could hurt him. Relax, Torel. He's my responsibility, not yours. And no, his parents don't know he's here."

"Parents?" Torel asked, already thankful that

whatever Vadir said next, it wasn't his responsibility to deal with it.

"My guest is Prince Radek, youngest son of the rulers of the Romaki Snow Dragon clan."

"Has anyone ever mentioned that you're a lunatic with the ethics of starving *paka*?"

Vadir laughed. "It's been mentioned once or twice." He rose from his chair and walked around Torel's small office to clasp his shoulder in a firm grip. "I appreciate you making time to see me today, with everything that's going on."

"Always. You're about to become a father for the first time, and your baby will have parents from two different species. Questions and concerns are to be expected. Anything you or Lisa need, you are always welcome to speak with me." He might never have children of his own, but Torel took great pride in knowing that the royal family had expanded his duties to include overseeing the pregnancy and eventual delivery of every child with a human mother. He would train others as plans progressed, but for now, he was the one everyone would come to. This would be his legacy.

Vadir said his goodbyes and departed, leaving Torel alone. Soon, he'd be on his way to Earth with the rest of the royal party. This was probably the last time he'd have peace and quiet until they returned to Pyros. The entire ship would soon be full of newly mated couples in the thrall of the Scorching, followed by all of the males, and no doubt some of the females, manifesting their ability to control fire. He was expecting to deal with more than a few minor burns, strains, and exhaustion by the time things settled down.

Today was a good day for Pyros. After years of desperate research, they still hadn't determined why there were so few females born each generation. Now, they had the human females to help restore the balance. In a few generations, the balance would be restored. It was a historic moment, and he was pleased to be part of it. He had no time for a mate of his own, but he didn't need a mate and offspring to make his mark. The Gods had provided him another way…even if the queen had insisted he register as a potential match. Thankfully, there was no match for him in the database. He had too much to do to be distracted by a mate of his own.

He ran a hand over his bearded jaw. He'd grown the beard while on vacation and kept it because his mother had liked it. She worried about him. Flames, she worried about all her children, but as the oldest, Torel seemed to garner more of her concern than the others.

"You look tired," she'd told him during their last day together. "Not your body, but your soul. You push yourself too hard. Find something that makes you happy and indulge yourself once in a while. There's more to life than work, 'Rel. Your father and I are grateful for all you've done for us, and so very proud of you. It's time to take care of yourself."

He pondered his mother's words as he got to his feet and headed for the door that led to his private quarters. It was good advice, but he'd spent most of his adult life working toward two goals: excelling in his career, and making sure that his parents would spend the rest of their lives financially secure. Now he'd achieved those goals, he had no idea how to switch gears, and he didn't plan on trying. He had a new goal, now. Do all he could to ensure his race continued.

RADEK

Star-crossed Alien Mail Order Brides #6

What do you do when your friend's planet runs out of women? Join them for takeout, of course.

Radek is a prince with a problem. He wants to see the galaxy, but an ancient law forbids any member of the Romaki Dragon Clans from ever leaving their planet. So, what's a Romaki Snow Dragon to do? Defy the law, hop a ride with a friend, and head for the far side of the galaxy, that's what.

As the Pyrosians prepare to claim their mates, all Radek has to do is sit back, enjoy the party, and keep one little promise – no shifting into a dragon while he's visiting Earth. What could be simpler?

This book contains a sassy chef whose dreams just went up in flames, and a runaway prince who thought he was escaping his destiny...until she dropped right into his claws.

Susan lives out on the Canadian west coast surrounded by open water, dear family, and good friends. She's jumped out of perfectly good airplanes on purpose and accidentally swum with sharks on the Great Barrier Reef.

If the world ends, she plans to survive as the spunky, comedic sidekick to the heroes of the new world, because she's too damned short and out of shape to make it on her own for long.

You can find out more about Susan and her books here:
www.susanhayes.ca